Standing close to Sloan and watching him loosen his necktie caused a thrilling response, a trembling from deep inside.

Maybe the danger had cranked her endorphins into high gear. Maybe his protective nature turned her on. Or maybe the timing was right. Whatever the reason, Brooke wanted him.

With a gentle caress, he brushed a wisp of hair off her cheek and tucked it behind her ear. The silver facets in his gray eyes sparked and shimmered. Whether this was magic or some kind of delusion, she liked it and leaned even closer to him, close enough that she could smell the smoke from the explosion that still clung to his clothes. The danger was real. She shouldn't allow herself to be distracted. But their bodies were almost touching.

THE GIRL WHO COULDN'T FORGET

USA TODAY Bestselling Author

CASSIE MILES

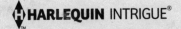

HARLEQUIN INTRIGUE®

To all the girls who survive and thrive in spite of tragedy.
And, as always, to Rick.

ISBN-13: 978-1-335-64074-1

The Girl Who Couldn't Forget

Copyright © 2019 by Kay Bergstrom

Recycling programs
for this product may
not exist in your area.

HARLEQUIN®

™ www.Harlequin.com

Printed in U.S.A.

Cassie Miles, a *USA TODAY* bestselling author, lives in Colorado. After raising two daughters and cooking tons of macaroni and cheese for her family, Cassie is trying to be more adventurous in her culinary efforts. She's discovered that almost anything tastes better with wine. When she's not plotting Harlequin Intrigue books, Cassie likes to hang out at the Denver Botanic Gardens near her high-rise home.

Books by Cassie Miles

Harlequin Intrigue

Mountain Midwife
Sovereign Sheriff
Baby Battalion
Unforgettable
Midwife Cover
Mommy Midwife
Montana Midwife
Hostage Midwife
Mountain Heiress
Snowed In
Snow Blind
Mountain Retreat
Colorado Wildfire
Mountain Bodyguard
Mountain Shelter
Mountain Blizzard
Frozen Memories
The Girl Who Wouldn't Stay Dead
The Girl Who Couldn't Forget

Visit the Author Profile page at Harlequin.com.

CAST OF CHARACTERS

Justin Sloan—FBI Special Agent Sloan responds to a complaint about harassing phone calls, uncovers a murder and finds himself partnered with a former victim who is smart, beautiful and strictly off-limits.

Brooke Josephson—Twelve years ago, Brooke was kidnapped along with five others and held for almost a year. In addition to horrifying memories, she's compulsively tidy and obsessive about adherence to the rules.

The Hardy Dolls—Martin Hardy is serving a 138-year sentence in prison for the kidnapping of six girls with black hair and blue eyes. Their captivity was twelve years ago.

Peter Channing—When he was eleven years old, Peter visited the Hardy Dolls with his uncle Martin. He cared deeply for them...perhaps too much.

Nick Brancusi—The documentarian made a lucrative film with the Dolls twelve years ago and wants to do an update using publicity from Layla's murder.

Tom Lancaster—The attorney for the Hardy Dolls is supposed to manage finances and advise them in bad situations. The murder is an indication that he's failed at his job.

Chapter One

The petunias were dead. That was the first thing Brooke Josephson noticed when she parked at the curb. Two months ago when she'd planted the flowers, her intention was to brighten up this dull brick building and make it into a more welcoming place for Franny. Instead, the yard had become a petunia graveyard with the tortured faces of faded purple, yellow and pink blooms staring helplessly. Withered leaves reached out in silent entreaty. All they'd needed was a splash of water. August in Denver could be hot and dry, but this wasn't the blazing Sahara.

Brooke leaped from her SUV and hurried along the sidewalk. The dead petunias were a bad omen—not enough to push her into a panic attack, but close. She had the symptoms: labored breathing, tremors, accelerated pulse and more. She paused. *Slow down. Shake it off.* At a more controlled pace, she proceeded toward the front door of her friend's one-bedroom at the end of a one-story, L-shaped apartment complex.

She never should have expected Franny to take care of the plants. Her friend's life was a wild, erratic whirl, and she'd never change. Why should she? If she was happy with chaos, so be it. Brooke loved her crazy friend like the little sister she'd never had. They even resembled each other. *Of course we look alike. He chose us for our black hair and blue eyes.*

It had been twelve years, but she remembered every detail. Her past was inescapable.

As she stepped onto the concrete stoop, she checked her precision quartz wristwatch. Twenty-seven minutes ago, she'd gotten Franny's call and had responded ASAP. She'd logged off her computer, dashed to her car, checked her GPS and adjusted her route to avoid the traffic slowdown for repairs on Alameda.

And here she stood, worried and scared. But ready to save the day if need be.

She punched the doorbell and called out, "Franny, it's me. Open up."

Most likely, this was a lot of fuss about nothing. If so, she'd bite her tongue and wouldn't scold. Extra caution was better than ignoring potential signs of danger, even though Brooke hated to waste time with unnecessary disruptions. Sometimes she could go a full week without leaving her house. Some people—including FBI Agent George Gimbel and her therapist—thought her behavior was borderline agoraphobic, but they didn't understand the importance of organization. There was no such thing as being too efficient.

From inside the apartment, she heard her friend chattering in a high-pitched jumble of words. She was answered by a man's rumbling voice. That wasn't right! Franny didn't date. She had no male relatives.

Brooke whipped her phone from the pocket of her khaki shorts and hit the emergency call button. *Better safe than sorry.* She unzipped her fanny pack and wrapped her fingers around the palm-size canister of pepper spray. "Franny, are you okay?"

She heard someone moving across the hardwood floor inside the apartment with a heavy tread; it must be the man. He was coming toward her. The pepper spray trembled in her hand. *I can handle this.* She had to. Nobody else would protect her and the people she loved. With the screen door open, she balanced on the balls of her feet— ready for action and glad that she'd worn sneakers instead of sandals. She braced herself. The first move would be hers.

The green-painted door was opened by a tall, dark-haired man in a suit.

Her phone squawked as the 911 operator answered, "Hello, what is your emergency?"

"You called the police," the man said.

Though law enforcement had failed her many times, Brooke needed backup. She shouted Franny's address at the phone and added, "We need help. Hurry."

"That's not necessary," he said.

"Where's my friend? What have you done to Franny?"

"Take it easy." He slid his hand inside his jacket. "Everything is fine."

Really? Then why are you reaching for a gun? She sprayed a blast of pepper spray. He dodged and threw up his arm for protection, but she knew that she'd scored a partial hit. While he winced and squinted, she darted into the apartment and positioned herself for another, more devastating blow.

"Brooke, stop!" Franny rushed from the back of the apartment. "What are you doing?"

"Taking care of this creep," she said.

She fired a karate kick at his knee and missed. Her next attempt aimed at his groin.

Her foot shot toward him. Before it connected, he grabbed her ankle and held on. It was all she could do not to lose her balance.

He held a wallet with his credentials toward her. "FBI."

"Let go of my leg!"

"Are you going to kick at me again?"

"Not if I don't need to." She brandished her pepper spray. "Don't try anything."

He dropped her ankle. "I ought to arrest you for assaulting a federal officer."

"Everybody please settle down," Franny said as she stepped between them. "Agent Sloan, you're not going to arrest anybody. Brooke, don't be a brat."

Oh, this was rich. The wildly irresponsible Franny Hennessey was telling her not to misbehave. As far as Brooke knew, that badge was a fake. If he was really a fed, he should have showed his credentials the minute he opened the door. Okay, maybe that was what he tried to do. Maybe this was as much her fault as his. Still, she said, "I'm not going to apologize."

"Don't care."

He glared at her through his right eye. The left squeezed shut, though the redness that came in reaction to the spray spread across his throat and stopped at his cheekbone. The blotch looked painful. "If you please," she said, "I'd like a closer look at that badge."

Without relinquishing his grasp on his wallet, he held his ID inches away from her nose. The documents appeared to be official. She read his name: Special Agent Justin Sloan.

She didn't usually make mistakes like this. Assaulting a fed? She placed her hand on her chest and felt the drumming of her heartbeat. Her adrenaline was running high, which wasn't a bad feeling, but not a good one, either. If she'd been home right now, she'd be opening mail and eat-ing her midafternoon snack of fruit and crackers. Instead, everything was up in the air.

She turned to her friend. "Why is he here?"

"I contacted him."

"Why?"

She shrugged. "I was trying to get ahold of Agent Gimbel. Remember him? The guy who handled our case?"

"Of course I remember." He was a kind man who had taken a genuine interest. She hoped nothing bad had happened to him. "Why couldn't he come?"

"Gimbel retired. The FBI office sent Sloan instead."

He pointed to Brooke's phone, which was still connected to an emergency operator asking questions. "Are you going to talk to her?"

This situation just got worse and worse. She'd requested emergency assistance, and she knew from past experience that nothing would divert the officers from coming to her aid. Rather than wasting time with long explanations to the dispatcher, she disconnected the call. Another rule broken.

Sloan asked, "Franny, do you have milk?"

Her ingenuous blue eyes opened wide. "Are you thirsty?"

"He wants milk to counteract the sting of the capsaicin in the pepper spray," Brooke explained as she snapped the cover onto the small canister and returned it to her fanny pack, where she also kept a supply of medicated wipes to use in case the pepper spray got onto her fingers. She opened the package, took out a wipe and handed it to Sloan before using one on her own hands. "Water is ineffective in washing off the oil-based propylene glycol."

"About that milk," Sloan repeated.

"Come with me," Franny said as she scampered barefoot toward the arched doorway leading to the kitchen. "I always have milk for the cats. Don't worry, I don't give them much. It's not healthy, you know. But they do love it."

Brooke trailed behind Special Agent Sloan and Franny, whose curly black hair bounced around her elfin face. For some unfathomable reason, she was wearing a purple sequin tiara. In her paisley-patterned yoga shorts and pink T-shirt with a sparkly unicorn on the front, she looked childlike and vulnerable. Actually, she was only four years younger than Brooke, who was twenty-six but felt like she'd already lived three lifetimes. No tiaras for her. She kept her long hair slicked back in a no-nonsense ponytail, which she twisted into a bun.

Her attention shifted to Sloan. He was tall, approximately seven inches over her five and a half feet, and he appeared to be in good physical condition. His gray suit jacket fit neatly across the wide expanse of his shoulders. There was something disturbing about the way he moved. Athletic and masculine, he seemed to exude confidence. Or was it arrogance? Either way, his presence unnerved her.

When she looked away from him, her gaze ricocheted around Franny's small apartment, where the decor was based on clutter, half-finished projects and more clutter. Brooke counted no fewer than four cats. The table in the dining area was covered with stacks of unopened mail, multicolored scraps of fabric and a sparkling array of beaded jewelry. Beside the table was a wicker basket of unfolded laundry that a fat gray-and-white cat was using as a bed. A teetering tower of books lurked in the corner. Instead of a curtain, Tibetan prayer flags draped across the dining room window, offering an alarmingly clear view of the sidewalk outside. Any passerby could easily see into the house. The security here was even worse than her last place.

In the kitchen, dirty dishes filled one side of the double sink. Half-eaten meals were scattered across the counter. Brooke couldn't help herself. She started washing the dishes.

"What are you doing?" Franny asked.

They'd had this conversation a hundred times before. "Left-out food attracts mice. I'll have this cleaned up in a sec."

"Don't bother." Franny laughed and pointed to

a black cat and a calico. "My mousers will protect me from varmints."

"Do any of these cats actually belong to you?"

"I don't own them, if that's what you mean."

As soon as Franny moved into a neighborhood, she made a point of befriending the local feline population. Brooke never knew from whence the cats came or where they went or why they liked to hang out with her friend. Maybe they recognized a kindred spirit.

"If you're looking for something to do, take care of him." Franny pointed to Agent Sloan, who had found a carton of milk in the fridge. "You broke him. You should fix him."

There was a certain amount of logic in what she said. *If Franny is making sense, I must be losing my mind.* Brooke directed Agent Sloan toward a straight-back chair beside a table where pots, pans and a basket full of green glass baubles took up most of the space. She took the carton from him, searched the cabinets for a clean bowl and poured the milk. While trying to find a fresh dish towel in the drawers, she said, "Take off your jacket, and be careful where you touch. The left sleeve probably has pepper spray on it."

He removed the holster clipped to his belt and placed his gun on the table next to the baubles. Then he peeled off his jacket and folded it into a neat package, which he stuck into a paper grocery bag that Franny handed him. The strip-tease didn't end there. He loosened his necktie. "I should probably take off my shirt, too."

Her already-speeding pulse jolted into high gear. "By all means, take off the shirt. Your collar might be...compromised."

Being careful to avoid handling the collar, he removed the short-sleeved cotton shirt. He wasn't wearing anything underneath. His nicely muscled chest showed off his tan.

Her fingers itched with an unexpected urge to rake though his black chest hair and slide over those taut pecs. *Snap out of it!* True, it had been a long time since she'd been this close to a half-naked man, but she wasn't the type to get all hot and bothered. Self-control was her middle name. With the bowl of milk and dish towel in hand, she approached the chair where he had taken a seat.

"Tilt your head up and to the right," she said.

His gaze connected with hers and...her heart stopped. Held in suspended animation, she couldn't breathe, couldn't move. Her ears were ringing. This wasn't a panic attack; it was something different, something she'd never experienced before. She blinked until her vision was clear and she found herself staring into the most fascinating eyes. They were deep set and gray with glittering facets of silver and green. His angular cheekbones matched a square jaw. His face was saved from severity by an ironic twist of his mouth. He had the kind of lips that were meant for kissing. Not that she was an expert. Her social life was only slightly more interesting than Franny's.

Her friend spoke up. "I'll see if I can find something for Sloan to wear."

"Excellent idea," Brooke said.

In an uncharacteristically clumsy manner, she swabbed the milk on the red blotches near his left ear. Excess from the dish towel dripped down his chest. She reached out with her bare hand to wipe it away. As soon as her fingers touched his flesh, a jolt of electricity traveled up her hand to her arm, then across her shoulder and down her chest, where it zapped her heart like a cardiovascular defibrillator. She jumped back. The milk spilled.

Breathlessly, she said, "No use crying over that."

He took the bowl from her. "Maybe I should do this myself."

"Yes, that would be easier." Aware that they were alone in the kitchen, she stepped back. This federal agent was a clear and present danger to her mental stability. "Have you spoken to Franny about why she called the FBI?"

"I have."

"Would you care to share that information?"

"She was trying to contact your mutual friend Layla and couldn't reach her." He dabbed at his cheek with the milk. "The text messages to her weren't answered. The phone calls went straight to voice mail."

"It's not unusual for Layla to go off the grid, and it's hardly a reason to call in the FBI." Brooke eyed him suspiciously. "You're not telling me everything, are you?"

"Franny's fears appear to be connected to what happened twelve years ago."

She didn't want to hear about this but had to know. "Tell me."

"Wait!" Franny dashed into the room with a crocheted poncho that she threw toward Sloan. She turned to Brooke. "Maybe we should forget about this. I'm feeling lots better, and I don't want you to get all freaked out."

Too late. Brooke was verging on a full-blown panic attack. She had to get this over with and go home. "You've got to tell me."

"Are you okay? You look kind of feverish."

"She's right," Sloan said. "Maybe you should sit."

As if she needed advice from a half-naked fed? "Will you excuse us, please?"

Without waiting for an answer, she dragged her friend through the messy front room into the equally cluttered bedroom, where she closed the door. Fearing she might pass out, Brooke lowered herself onto the edge of the unmade bed, trying not to think of this mattress as a breeding ground for bacteria and dust mites. She concentrated on breathing slowly, struggling not to drown in the fierce torrents that churned inside her.

Franny sat beside her. "I was scared about how you might react. That's why I didn't call you first. I figured Gimbel could look into stuff and make it all better."

But Gimbel had retired. Brooke asked, "What kind of stuff?"

"For the past couple of days, maybe a week, I've been getting phone calls from a number I didn't recognize."

"And?"

"They were weird."

Extracting information from her was like peeling an artichoke one leaf at a time. Brooke turned her head and focused on the blue of Franny's eyes—a color that was almost identical to her own. "Why did you think the calls were weird?"

"My voice mail picked up a couple of them. I can play them back."

"Maybe later." She didn't want to spend any more time here than absolutely necessary. Either there was reason for concern or not. "For now, just tell me."

"His voice was whispery." Her eyes lowered, and she sucked on her lower lip. "He said that little ladies who didn't do as they were told would be punished."

The terrible warning—one she'd heard before—set off a screeching alarm in Brooke's brain. *No, no, no, no, I don't want to remember.* "What else?"

"My finger." She held up her left hand. The little finger had been severed at the second joint. "He asked if I missed my finger."

"It wasn't him," Brooke said firmly. "Martin Hardy is locked away in prison for life. He can never touch you again."

"That's what Sloan said. And he promised to check on the other girls, to make sure they were safe. That's why I wanted you to come over to meet him." Though tears swamped her eyes, she forced a wobbly smile. "He's kind of gorgeous, huh?"

"I hadn't noticed."

"Yeah, you did. You were blushing."

Brooke scowled as she rose from the bed and paced on the small portion of floor that wasn't covered by a jumble of discarded clothing. Recently, she'd experienced a few odd incidents herself. Twice during the past week her car alarm had gone off, even though it was parked in the attached garage. She'd never found an explanation, but it hadn't seemed particularly threatening until now. "Was there anything other than phone calls?"

"Should I be scared?"

"I don't know."

"Do you think it's a copycat?" Her voice went high and nervous. "Our case was written up in the newspapers and online. And there's that movie guy who wants all six of us to get together for a follow-up story."

"His documentary is never going to happen." She'd vowed to sue the pants off anybody who tried to take advantage of them. "Until we have some answers, you should stay at my house."

"Why?"

Not wanting to get Franny riled up with more criticism, Brooke didn't mention the lack of security in her apartment or the uncurtained windows that were open to public view or the fact that cats could dart in and out at will. This place was unsafe. "If something is truly wrong, we need to stick together."

The doorbell rang, and she heard Agent Sloan cross the front room. He called out, "I'll answer it."

The fact that there was an armed federal agent in the other room reassured her. She pulled Franny to her feet. "Where's your suitcase?"

"I don't want to pack. Do I have to?"

"Not a problem. I've got everything at my house that you might need." With a renewed sense of purpose and a laser focus on home, she propelled her friend through the bedroom door. "Grab your keys and let's get out of here."

In the front room, Brooke would have preferred to make a beeline for the exit, but Sloan and two uniformed officers blocked the way. With his holster clipped to his belt and Franny's too-small poncho covering his shoulders, Sloan looked like a deranged outlaw. She wondered how he had explained his outfit to the cops who had arrived in response to her 911 call.

She checked her watch. Thirty-three minutes had elapsed since she'd spoken to the emergency operator. If this had been an attack by a homicidal maniac, they'd all be dead by now. Nonetheless, she thanked the officers for coming and apologized for the false alarm.

To Sloan, she said, "I'm taking Franny to my house. She'll be safe with me. Do you plan to investigate the phone calls she received?"

"Yes," he said curtly.

"Please keep me informed."

Franny popped up beside them holding a black plastic garbage bag filled with the scraps and glitter from the table. Her fears seemed to have disappeared. She was beaming. Brooke envied her friend's resilience, even though she didn't completely believe that bubbly smile.

Before they could escape out the door, one of the uniformed officers stepped forward. "I know you," he said. "Matter of fact, I recognize both of you with the black hair and blue eyes. You're two of the Hardy Dolls."

The emotions Brooke had been holding back erupted. Every muscle in her body tensed. Twelve years ago, six girls—all with black hair and sad blue eyes—had been abducted from their foster homes by a psychopath named Martin Hardy. He had held them captive in an isolated house in the mountains where they'd been shackled, drugged, starved and brutalized. He'd done unspeakable things.

"Hardy Dolls," the cop repeated. "I'm right, aren't I?"

She despised the demeaning nickname the press had labeled them with. *Hardy Dolls* sounded like the six of them were a soccer team or a rock group, instead of the cruel truth that nobody wanted to face—they were throwaway foster kids who nobody missed and nobody searched for. They'd had to save themselves.

"We're not dolls. Not now. Not ever."

Without another word, she turned on her heel and stormed out the front door. *I never should have left my house.*

Chapter Two

Yesterday, when Brooke dashed out the door from Franny's apartment, Sloan hadn't made the mistake of thinking that she was running away. Fear hadn't been her motivation. Anger had driven her. She'd left to avoid a fight, and he'd been grateful. Unless he missed his guess, Brooke Josephson was a formidable adversary who might have eviscerated that cop with the big mouth.

In order to verify that opinion and learn more about the victimology of the young women who had been kidnapped, he paid a midmorning visit to George Gimbel. At the retired agent's home in the foothills west of town, the two men sat on rocking chairs on the front porch, drinking black coffee and watching the pecking chickens outside their coop. A dappled, swayback mare with a big belly that mimicked the girth of her owner grazed in the corral attached to the small barn. Though Sloan could make out the downtown Denver skyline in the faraway distance, the peaceful setting made him feel like he'd gone back in time to the Old West.

Gimbel took off his cowboy hat and dragged his fingers through his unruly gray hair. "There hasn't been a day in the past twelve years that I haven't thought about those women. Never felt like we did right by them."

Sloan had read the files on the case. "From the record, it looks like you were thorough."

"Oh, yeah, the proper forms were filed. But when it came to an investigation? *Nada.*" His thumb and forefinger formed a zero. "They were abducted over a period of four or five months. Six girls went missing, one after another. Where were the cops? Where was the FBI? We dropped the ball. And why? Well, these were all foster kids— teenagers or younger. Everybody assumed they were runaways."

All too often, victims fell between the cracks. These women had been taken from different homes that were as far apart as Colorado Springs to the south and Cheyenne, Wyoming, to the north. They hadn't known each other, and there hadn't seemed to be a connection…except for one. Sloan pointed it out. "If someone in law enforcement had lined up their photos and noticed the similarities in appearance, they would have paid more attention."

"That's exactly what happened when the public learned about the kidnappings—intense publicity. Some of the victims were traumatized by the spotlight."

"Like Brooke."

"I'm not so sure about that," Gimbel said. "She's hard to read."

Sloan remembered her trembling hands, rapid breathing and darting gaze. "From the minute we met, it seemed like she was about to have a panic attack."

"But she didn't."

"Oh. Hell. No. She blasted me with pepper spray and tried to kick me in the groin."

Gimbel chuckled. "Brooke avoids confrontation, but she never backs down."

"How did the FBI get involved in the case?"

"When the women escaped, they went to the Jefferson County police, who realized that they were dealing with kidnapping. Since two states— Colorado and Wyoming—were involved, JeffCo was only too happy to pass this big, fat, complicated case to us, where it landed in my lap." He leaned back and folded his hands across his gut. "I'll never forget the first time I saw all six of them together. Skinny little things with black hair and blue eyes, they looked so much alike that they could have been sisters. Actually, two of them are identical twins."

"Hardy Dolls," Sloan said.

"Brooke hated when the media started using that moniker, and I don't blame her. If that girl is a doll, she's sure as hell an action figure. To survive in captivity, she had to be tough. To engineer an escape with five other girls, she had to be smart."

Sloan agreed. In the testimony given by the others, it was obvious how much they respected Brooke. Their descriptions of the escape showed an extreme degree of planning from the fourteen-year-old. Oddly, Brooke had said very little. Her statement was limited to short answers and claims that she didn't remember. A complex woman, there was something about her that fascinated him. "She took charge, but she wasn't the oldest."

"Layla was sixteen."

"And Layla Tierney is the reason I'm following up. When Franny started getting threatening phone calls, she contacted the others to find out if they'd received similar anonymous contacts. She never reached Layla."

"She disappears from time to time," Gimbel said. "Brooke will know how to find her."

He was glad for another reason to be in touch with her. "I appreciate any advice. Victimology is new to me. My training put more emphasis on the criminals and psychopaths."

"Three months ago, when you got assigned to the Denver office, they said we were lucky to have you." There was a hint of bitterness in his tone. "You're only a few credits short of a PhD in psychology. Is that right?"

Sloan nodded. "I'm working on my dissertation."

"To tell you the truth, I'm more impressed with the fact that you served in the navy."

"Which is how I paid for college." He hadn't joined the navy out of a sense of duty or patriotism, but he'd gotten more from his service than he ever expected. His dad had told him that the US Navy would teach him to be a man. In this case, Dad might have been right.

"I never enlisted," Gimbel said, "but I figure I paid my dues with a twenty-seven-year career in the FBI."

Sloan rose from his chair and went to the banister, where he watched the hens and avoided making direct eye contact with Gimbel. He didn't want their meeting to turn into a confrontation between the grizzled old veteran and the smart-ass college boy. Not that he was a kid at thirty-two.

"I've only got a couple years' experience in the field," he said. "Dealing with six different victims who have each developed their own coping behaviors is complicated to say the least. Your insights would really help."

"Let's get to it," he said.

"From your notes, it's clear they're all experiencing a degree of post-traumatic stress."

"You don't need a PhD to figure that out." Gimbel was kind enough not to scoff. Instead, he took a sip of his coffee. "Give me your profile of Franny."

He didn't like making a snap diagnosis but didn't have time to analyze his subject. Unlike therapy, profiling drew broad conclusions. "The clutter in her house and immature behavior points to ADD. She hides her feelings behind a bright, happy exterior—shiny enough to deflect close examination. Inside, she's a drama queen."

The older man nodded. "You got that right."

"Not being able to contact Layla for a few days shouldn't have been a big deal, but Franny was extremely agitated. The anonymous phone calls triggered her fears."

"Tell me about the calls."

"There were references to her time in captivity." Sloan repeated the words verbatim. "Everything the caller said was public knowledge."

"Did you check out the number?"

"It traced to a burner phone. Even the dumbest perverts use throwaways."

"But you investigated. Good."

Sloan was glad he hadn't immediately dismissed Franny's complaint. As Gimbel had pointed out, the law enforcement system hadn't paid enough attention when these women disappeared the first time. He refused to be the guy who failed them again. "I see two possibilities.

The first is that Franny is getting targeted by a prison groupie who idolizes Martin Hardy. He's a copycat and bears watching but probably won't go further than crank calls. The other, more disturbing scenario suggests unresolved issues from the original crime. In your reports, you listed other men who knew Hardy and might have assisted in the abductions."

"There's no shortage of creeps out there," Gimbel said. "I hope Franny's fears are nothing but a feather on the wind, but you can't take that chance. It's your job to protect them."

"That's what you did."

"Damn right," Gimbel said. "I had to be sure they weren't just dumped back into the foster care system. And I got a lawyer to manage their interests. I'll give you his name."

Gimbel was turning out to be a valuable resource. Sloan folded his arms across his chest and leaned against the banister. "Tell me about Brooke."

AFTER A LATE LUNCH, Sloan parked his SUV outside Brooke's gleaming white stucco house with a red tile roof. Hers was one of several Spanish Mission-style homes in this architecturally diverse urban neighborhood. The two-story house was surrounded by a tidy lawn, perfectly trimmed shrubs and colorful flower beds. And the place was well protected. He spotted two security cameras. One was mounted over the front door. Another peered down from the attached garage. Wrought iron latticework—in a decorative pattern—shielded the door and the arched windows on the first floor.

As soon as he exited his vehicle, the August heat hit him like a blast furnace. He straightened his striped necktie, smoothed the wrinkles from his linen suit jacket and tried not to sweat. He was eager to see Brooke again. Her personality—an impossible combination of fire and ice—fascinated him.

Not that their relationship could be anything but professional. She was a witness, possibly a victim, and he had to keep his distance. His reason for being here and talking to her was to determine his starting point in this widely disparate investigation. In addition to the anonymous phone calls to Franny, threats had been made to the other women. He needed Brooke's sensible approach to sort the real from the unreal, ultimately making sense of the situation. And, first and foremost, he needed to locate Layla.

As soon as he rang the bell, Franny yanked the door open and dived into his arms. After a giant hug—so much for professional distance—she bounced away from him. This young woman was as energetic and enthusiastic as a puppy looking for a pat on the head.

"Hey there," she said brightly. "You did a

pretty great job of contacting everybody. They all called me, except for Layla."

"You said Brooke would know how to find her."

Franny grabbed his hand and pulled him into a two-story foyer with a terra-cotta floor and a curved staircase on the right. Compared to the hot weather outside, the house was cool and serene. He felt like he'd walked into a shaded glen in a perfectly organized forest.

"Those two, Brooke and Layla, are birdies of a feather," Franny said. "Both really smart and focused and, you know, tidy."

He grinned. Franny's casual description matched Gimbel's more technical analysis of OCD tendencies brought on by post-traumatic stress. "They like to keep things orderly."

"And I make them crazy," she confided.

An alarm shrieked, and Franny ran to a keypad near the door, where she punched random numbers. "I forgot to turn it off. Oh my God, that's loud. Can you help me?"

Brooke charged into the foyer. "Step away from the keypad."

Franny leaped backward as Brooke plugged in the numbers to turn off the alarm. She placed a cell phone in Franny's hand. "The security people are going to call and ask if we need help. Do you remember what you're supposed to tell them?"

"The code words," she said. "Happy trails to you."

"And then?"

"They'll tell me to repeat, but this time I'll say, 'Hi-ho, Silver, and away.'"

When Franny left to handle the call from the security service, Brooke turned toward him. "Good afternoon, Special Agent Sloan. You didn't mention that you were coming over when you called earlier."

"I was afraid you'd bar the door."

A hint of a smile twitched the corner of her rosebud mouth. If she ever actually laughed, he suspected she'd have dimples. "Given our previous encounter," she said, "I understand."

This was the cool version of Brooke Josephson. Her raging tension was gone, and she appeared to be completely in control, probably because she was at home. Safely tucked away in her lair, Brooke could relax and be comfortable. She was shoeless and bare-legged, wearing an untucked dark blue shirt and knee-length white shorts. Her black hair tumbled loosely to her shoulders.

Though he could have spent an enjoyable few moments studying her features—the classic nose, sculpted brow, wide forehead and pointed chin— Sloan went straight to business. He reached into the inner pocket of his navy blue blazer and extracted a small spiral notebook. "I know you don't like to waste time, so I made a list."

"Efficient." She gave a small nod of approval. "Would you like something to drink? Water? Juice?"

"A glass of water would be fine."

Franny bounded back into the foyer and returned the phone to Brooke. "I handled the security call. This is the third time, so I think I'm getting the hang of it."

He gave her a smile. "Mind if I ask you a question?"

"Shoot." She mimicked a gunslinger doing a fast draw—an image this little pixie couldn't really pull off.

"You answered the doorbell as soon as it rang. Were you watching from a window?"

"We're way more techie than that." With a giggle, she picked up a computer tablet that was sitting on a rectangular wooden side table below the staircase. Franny tapped in a code and showed him a screen divided into four separate video feeds. "These are live pictures from the three cameras outside the house and the one in the office. I saw you park and watched you walk to the door."

"Impressive," he murmured.

"The cameras might seem excessive," Brooke said, "but I work from home, and I have a lot of very expensive electronic equipment to protect."

"No need to explain. I like all this tech stuff."

"And yet you carry a spiral notebook."

Not exactly a subtle put-down. His attempt to bond with her by pretending they shared an interest in electronics had fallen flat. She wasn't buying it. He stifled an urge to explain his lousy relationship with computers. Giving her too much information gave her an edge, and he needed to stay in charge. An uncomfortable silence filled the entryway.

"Wow," Franny said. "There's some real chemistry between you two. I mean, it's combustible. And that's my cue to leave you alone. Don't do anything I wouldn't."

He watched her scamper up the stairs to the second floor. "I understand that she's marching to her own drummer, but I don't know this tune."

"Franny has decided that you and I are some kind of match, and we should start dating. I told her it wasn't acceptable, not according to the rules."

"And I'll bet she doesn't care."

"Not a whit."

He followed Brooke as she bypassed the pristine living room, decorated in earthy Southwestern colors, and went down a corridor to the kitchen. The sleek black cabinets and polished marble countertops were clean and organized. Brooke had her life choreographed down to the smallest detail. "I have a question that isn't written down in my spiral notebook," he said. "You and Franny are very different in habit and temperament. How do you put up with her when she stays with you?"

"We have an agreement," she said. "No cats are allowed in the house. And her clutter is confined to the upstairs guest bedroom and attached bathroom."

"Does she follow those rules?"

"Not always, but I can't blame her for living her life the way she wants. Like the clown at the end of the circus procession, it's my job to follow the Franny parade and sweep up the mess after she rides past on a bejeweled elephant."

Her comparison surprised him. In no way did he think of Brooke as a clown. Playing the fool might hint at low self-esteem issues, but he was more interested in her willingness to set aside her own requirements for neatness when it came to someone she loved. She liked order but wasn't rigid about it.

She took two blue glasses from the shelf above the sink and filled them with purified water from a pitcher in the fridge. "What's first on your list?"

He made a point of consulting his notebook. "When we talked on the phone, you mentioned that your car alarm went off while it was parked in the garage. Now that I've seen your security precautions, I'm even more curious about how that could happen."

"I don't know." She stood behind the center island and slid the glass toward him. "I checked at the time. Nothing had fallen and bumped the SUV. All locks were secure."

"Did your cameras pick up any sign of an intruder?"

She shook her head. "The only explanation I've been able to come up with is a glitch of some sort. I'm not an expert in car mechanics."

When he'd talked to the other women, they had all reported similar issues that amounted to minor annoyances. One of them thought a man had been following her. Another reported personal items that had gone missing from her house, but she wasn't sure if she'd just misplaced them. The one who had left Denver and moved to Las Vegas mentioned that she was contacted three times by a documentary filmmaker.

He glanced at his list. "Have you had other threats?"

"Not recently. People have always wanted to get close to us, and they act like we're some kind of notorious celebrities." Anger wove through her voice. "In the early days after we escaped, there was a great deal of unwanted attention. For some reason, folks thought it was all right to call or write letters or walk up to us on the street as though we were old friends. Not exactly threatening, but I considered their behavior to be intrusive. I hated it."

"Gimbel said he put you in touch with a lawyer."

"Tom Lancaster," she said. "It was handy to

have his card to warn people away. And he was useful in other practical ways. He set up a fund for us to handle various donations. There was enough money to fund private school for Franny and the twins."

"What about you? You didn't return to high school."

"There was no way I'd go back and be gawked at. I got my GED and enrolled in community college. Layla did the same, and she continued to law school. She recently graduated and has been studying for the bar exam."

According to Gimbel, Brooke breezed through college, earning scholarships and completing her course work for a business degree before she was twenty. After an internship with an IT firm, she set up a home-based business doing medical and legal transcriptions. "You and Layla have much in common. Both intelligent. Both ambitious and successful."

She pushed a wing of black hair away from her face and gave him a smile. "You're a profiler, aren't you?"

"Not yet. But I've had psychological training."

"Well, you hit the jackpot with this case. Me and my friends are every shade of crazy."

Though he didn't approve of labels, he appreciated her relaxed attitude. Yesterday she'd been as prickly as a cactus. "Do you know how to reach Layla?"

"I tried. Yesterday Franny and I stopped by her apartment, and I tried to contact her on a computer link. I tried the link again, about three hours ago. No Layla."

"Would you give it another try?"

"Sure, come with me to my office." She gave him a more genuine smile, and her dimples appeared. "I'll send out the bat signal."

Sloan followed her down a corridor into a large room with a wall of file cabinets and three distinct workstations, each equipped with computers and ergonomic chairs. A wide window, covered with wrought iron grillwork, showed a shaded, verdant backyard with two peach trees and a vegetable garden.

He went to the window. "You grow your own food."

"Gimbel accused me of planting a garden so I wouldn't ever have to leave my house." She slid into place behind a computer. "He might be right. I love being able to step outside and pick a salad. My tomatoes this year have been brilliant."

He stood behind her so he could see the screen as her slender fingers danced across the keyboard, clicking icons and tapping in passcodes. "I'm not very computer savvy," he said.

"I guessed."

"Tell me what you're doing."

"This program activates a camera that provides a live feed from a one-room mountain cabin that

Layla and I share. We're both reclusive. Sometimes we need a hideout where we can be completely alone." She glanced over her shoulder at him. "Layla uses the cabin when she's studying. After a big work project, I like to go there to decompress."

"But you don't want to be completely out of touch," he said. "That's why you set up this system. What did you call it? The bat signal?"

"It's a safety concern," she said, "only to be used in urgent circumstances. Though I'm not sure this investigation rises to the level of emergency, I'll feel better after we've checked in with her."

When she tapped the final key, a picture appeared on the screen. He saw a wood-paneled room with a desk, a fireplace and a bed. The only light came from a window.

"There she is," Brooke said as she pointed to the bed.

He needed confirmation on where Layla had been and if she'd been threatened. "Can you talk to her through the live feed?"

"Sure." Loudly, she said, "Layla, it's me. Get up."

"Zoom in closer?"

"Come on, sleepyhead." Brooke tapped a few keys.

The screen filled with a close-up of Layla's image. Though her nightgown reached up to her chin, Sloan noticed the discoloration at her throat. Layla's face was drained of color. Her cheeks were hollow. She lay unnaturally still.

He'd witnessed enough autopsies to know that this woman would never respond to Brooke's calls for her to wake up.

Chapter Three

Riveted, Brooke stared at the screen, unwilling to believe what she was seeing. Layla, beautiful Layla, was carefully posed on the bed in the one-room cabin. Her head tilted to the right, toward the door and the kitchenette. Her shiny black hair fanned out on the pillowcase. Her pink gown was buttoned all the way up to her chin. The flowered peach comforter tucked under her arms had been smoothed to perfection, and her long fingers laced together below her breasts. Brooke stared at the plain gold band that gleamed from Layla's left hand—stared so hard that her eyes strained and began to water. *Not again.*

Twelve years ago, Layla was forced to be Hardy's bride. That had been her role in the sick little family he had created. Night after night, he'd come to her, demanding his rights as her husband. At first, Layla had screamed. And she must have struggled, because Brooke had heard the crashing around and had treated Layla's wounds the following day. Her blood had been literally on Brooke's hands.

After a while, Layla had given up and quit fighting. Her desperate cries had faded into quiet sobs. At the end of the seven months they were held captive, Layla's voice had been silent in the night.

Brooke buried her face in her hands. Layla didn't deserve an early death, not after what she'd survived. She'd worked so hard to get through law school. Her dream had been to defend other victims who had given up hope and had nowhere else to turn. Why had she been taken? Why? Brooke dropped her hands. There was no answer. Sometimes, life didn't make sense.

In a flat voice, she said, "Layla's dead."

"We don't know for sure."

Sloan didn't make the mistake of trying to comfort her with a touch or a pat on the shoulder or a hug. He kept his distance. *Smart man.* She could already feel her grief transforming into anger, and she might lash out at whatever or whoever was in her path. "I should call the sheriff."

"I'll handle it," he said. "Give me directions to the cabin or an address so I can contact the authorities and the ambulance."

She wrote the information on a sticky note. Her fingers trembled, but she took care to make her penmanship legible. "We don't have a spare key hidden at the cabin, and the windows are secure. Still, I'd appreciate if they don't break down the door."

"I'll pass that along."

He stepped away from the desk but didn't leave the office. Hovering in the doorway, he kept an eye on her. His voice was a smooth murmur as he made phone calls. She overheard him tell someone to treat the cabin like a crime scene.

The image on the computer screen wavered before her eyes, and she forced herself to inhale a steadying breath before she made a promise to Layla Tierney. "You will have justice, my sister. I will find the bastard who did this to you, and I will make him pay."

Adrenaline surged through her veins. *A wake-up call.* This sensation was unlike her panic attacks or the nervous tension that sapped her energy and left her paralyzed. She felt powerful, strong and filled with purpose. There was nothing more she could do for Layla, but she'd make sure the killer was caught and no one else came to harm.

With a few keystrokes, she exited the computer connection to the cabin. If Franny came in here and stumbled across the image of their dead friend, she'd be devastated. Brooke rose from behind her desk and confronted Sloan when he ended his call.

"I'm coming with you," she said.

"Please sit, Brooke. I need to ask you a few questions."

Still standing, she said, "We should get going."

"You tried to reach Layla at the cabin yesterday. What time?"

"It was after Franny and I left her apartment—between four thirty and four forty-five. The cabin was empty."

"And today?"

"It was three hours ago, before I made lunch. One of the twins contacted me, and I told her I'd check again." At the time, she hadn't been worried. Over the years, she'd grown complacent, believing all of them were safe and could lead relatively normal lives. *Clearly, a mistake.* "This was my fault. If I'd gone to the cabin this morning, I could have prevented Layla's murder."

"You don't know that."

"Based on the time I contacted her, she must have been killed during the three-hour window between eleven thirty and right now."

"I advise against making assumptions," he said in a firm voice that was both aggravating and authoritative. "Until we investigate and have evidence, we can't draw conclusions."

"But it's obvious."

"Think about it, Brooke." Rather than handling her with kid gloves, he seemed to be using a direct approach. "Did you see signs of violence in the cabin?"

She appreciated his candor. "There wouldn't be blood spatters if she was strangled."

"But she would have struggled," he said. "I see no defensive wounds on her hands or arms. No bruises or scratches. We don't know what happened. Or when. To determine the time of death, we need a coroner's report."

"You're right."

"She might have died elsewhere and been transported to the cabin."

Brooke was ashamed that she hadn't considered all those possibilities. Where was her brain? Her intelligence seemed to have deserted her at a moment when she needed to calm down and concentrate. Sloan was right when he told her not to base her thinking on unfounded suppositions, which was precisely why she needed to go to the crime scene and gather information. "Shouldn't we be going?"

"When was the last time you spoke to Layla?"

"I can check my phone records, but I think it was four days ago, on Monday. She'd made an appointment to look at a property she might lease as an office and wanted me to come." Brooke sat behind her desk, brought up her digital calendar and pointed to the notation. "See, right there. It was supposed to be tomorrow at ten in the morning. I should call and cancel."

Verifying a meeting with a property manager seemed trivial, but Brooke knew she'd make that call before the day was over. She was compelled to take care of details. Life went on even when Layla was dead. Oh, God, this was so unfair. Tears threatened, and she tossed her head, shaking them away. "I'm ready. We should go now."

"I can't take you with me, Brooke. Bringing a witness to a crime scene is against the rules."

The clever man already knew her well enough to present the argument that would be most persuasive. He was aware that she hated to disobey normal conventions. But her need to avenge her friend surpassed her habit of coloring inside the lines. She had to convince him.

"Lipstick," she said.

"What about lipstick?"

"Layla is wearing a particular color—Rosy Posey—that Hardy liked. She'd never choose that disgusting pinkness for herself. And the shiny, narrow wedding band is almost a perfect match for the one that Hardy forced her to wear." She could be straightforward, too. "I know more about Layla and the things that happened to us than anyone else. You need me. I can be a valuable asset in your investigation."

"And I'll review my findings with you. But you should stay here, where you're safe. It might be best for you and Franny and the others to go into protective custody."

"I won't object if you arrange for a patrol car to park outside and keep an eye on Franny."

"Consider it done."

"I'm going to the cabin. Either I can ride with you or I'll drive myself." She took a small key from the rectangular wooden pencil box on her desktop, unlocked the lower right drawer and took out her Glock 42 handgun in its holster. "Your choice, Sloan."

He approached her desk and stopped when he was close enough to reach out and snatch the weapon from her hand. "Do you have the necessary registration and permits?"

"I take the ownership of a weapon seriously," she said. "Not only have I gone through the certification and qualified as expert in marksmanship, but I have a shooting range in the basement for target practice."

His eyebrows lifted, and his gray eyes widened. "In the basement?"

"Soundproofed, of course." She'd managed to surprise him, and that pleased her.

"You don't need a gun," he said. "When we get to the cabin, there'll be several armed officers."

"When we get there…" She parroted his words, underlining his implied acceptance. He had almost agreed to bring her along. "I promise that I won't get in the way."

"Why does it feel like you tricked me?"

Before he changed his mind, she wanted to get

him out the door and into the car. Quickly, she slipped into her espadrilles under the desk. "I'm ready. Let's go."

"Leave the weapon here."

She weighed the alternatives. The gun made her feel safer, but she wanted Sloan on her side. Pushing him too hard might be a mistake. She returned the Glock to her desk drawer, locked it and grabbed her handy-dandy, all-purpose black fanny pack. "Do you have a problem with this?"

"Not if you keep your pepper spray in the holster."

After he called in a police car to guard the front door and she dashed upstairs to tell Franny to stay put, they were on their way.

FROM THE STREET in front of Brooke's house to the cabin was a drive that took seventy minutes, more or less. This afternoon would be more. Traffic snarls, detours and bumper-to-bumper jam-ups slowed their progress. Though impatient, Brooke was grateful for the extra time to figure out exactly what she was doing.

Her first instinct had been to launch herself into the investigation, even though she knew for a fact that impulsive actions were often regrettable. She'd be wise to trust the police and the FBI. After all, it was their job to nab murderers. Sloan would probably be the officer in charge, and he seemed competent.

She studied his profile as he drove. His firm jaw hinted at a determined attitude, and she hoped that trait held true, that he was unstoppable and wouldn't rest until he caught his man. But she knew better than to count on his physiognomy to understand his character. Hadn't the notorious serial killer Ted Bundy been an attractive man? She didn't know Sloan well enough to trust him.

He seemed to be a careful driver but had been talking on his hands-free phone the whole time they were in his SUV. He'd plugged the address for the cabin into his GPS and was relying on the dashboard information for directions rather than asking her. He probably thought he was being efficient. But he wasn't. If asked, she could have directed him to a shortcut that would have avoided the usual slowdown on Sixth.

Sloan ended his call and looked toward her. "I've asked Agent Gimbel to meet us at the cabin."

"Smart move." Not only had Agent Gimbel studied their case, but she'd be glad to see him. The older man was a reassuring presence.

"I have one more call."

"Take your time."

Brooke would have preferred being in charge. She never enjoyed riding in the passenger seat, but she forced herself to lean back and let the air-conditioning wash over her while she kept her mouth shut. When Sloan took a sharp left turn, she pinched her lips together to keep from blurting out her criticism of his momentarily inattentive driving. She closed her eyes.

Relaxation was impossible. The inside of her head filled with the image of Layla from the computer. Brooke popped her eyes open and blinked hard, hating that high-definition memory. *Why can't I just forget?*

Being too smart was a curse. She'd rather be blissfully dumb. *But not really.* She appreciated her intelligence. The secret was how to use it. Recalling what Sloan had said about details that might be clues, Brooke purposely brought back the vision.

Except for the garish pink lipstick, Layla hadn't seemed to be wearing much makeup, which was her preference. She seldom bothered with mascara and foundation, preferring a clean face and frequently washed hands. Her personal hygiene habits were even more compulsive than Brooke's. Had the person who murdered Layla known about that trait? Had he made sure that her hair was freshly washed? Her hands clean? Was he someone who knew her well? Or was he a stalker who had watched her for a long time?

She needed a profile of the killer. Supposedly, that branch of psychology was within the realm of Sloan's expertise. "We need to get started," she said, interrupting his phone call.

He excused himself to the person on the phone and looked at her. "Started with what?"

"The profile," she said. "I want a basis to work from."

Finally, the SUV hit a path of smooth, unobstructed highway as they approached the foothills. At the end of an arid summer, the vegetation was dull as dirt. He ended his phone call and said, "A profile isn't guaranteed to be accurate. It provides broad parameters of personality type and behavior."

"A parameter is just fine. Like I said, I want the profile as a basis—a starting point for the investigation."

"You can help me." He shot her a quick glance. "I can't pull a detailed profile out of my back pocket. I can start with gathering more information about Layla."

"Like what?" She gestured for him to speed it up. "Ask me questions."

"From reading Gimbel's files, I know that she was an orphan with no family ties."

"Like me." The demographic was the same. They were both orphans, but Layla's life was far more complicated. Her parents were both addicts who died together in a car accident when Layla was five or six years old. Brooke had been abandoned at birth—wrapped in a cheap blanket and left outside a fire station. "We both had lousy upbringings but were doing okay until we got kid-napped by a psycho. Move along."

"I'm sorry," he said.

The gentleness of his voice surprised her. She hadn't expected sympathy or empathy or what-ever this was. Her shields went up. "We're going to be at the cabin in twenty-five minutes or less. What else do you need to know?"

"Tell me about Layla's social life. Was she a party girl? Did she have a lot of boyfriends or only one special guy?"

"Parties and clubs weren't her thing. She didn't drink or do drugs. Two years ago, there was a guy in law school that she got serious about, but nobody recently."

"Online dating?"

"Never." Like her, Layla was protective of her privacy. "I don't understand all these questions about her. Shouldn't your profile focus on the murderer?"

"The victim comes first. Understanding why the killer attacked her can help in building a pro-file." Following the GPS directions, he made a right turn onto a secondary road that went deeper into the pine forests. "It might seem obvious to you that Layla's murder is tied to the abductions twelve years ago, but the scope of an investiga-tion is widespread. She might have been targeted by someone she knew at school."

"Then why would they put on that lipstick or the wedding ring?"

"The quick answer is that they were interested in her history and looked up the details on the computer, but there are many other possibilities."

"You're being thorough."

"That's right."

She nodded in approval. "I'll make a list of the men Layla dated in the past couple of years. And another list of professional contacts—people she's worked for, schoolmates, professors and mentors."

"Also doctors, therapists and your attorney," he said. "It'd help if you put it on a thumb drive so we can build a database."

"All those guys are suspects?"

"Most will be quickly eliminated, but it helps to cover all bases."

"You can turn off the GPS," she said. "We're here."

The cabin that she and Layla had purchased for their private hideaway perched among the trees on the side of a steep hill. The main road ascended the incline, and her driveway peeled off, cutting straight across the hill, forty-seven yards to her cabin. Several official-looking vehicles, including an ambulance, had gathered at the start of the asphalt driveway but hadn't driven up to the house.

She looked toward the house, where she

counted two men in sheriff's uniforms and one in a suit like Sloan. "Why didn't they drive closer?"

"They didn't want to disturb possible tire tracks or footprints."

The driveway was mostly asphalt, but there was dirt on either side. Again, she was impressed by the methodical approach used by law enforcement. She unfastened her seat belt and inhaled what she hoped would be a calming breath. In moments, the image on the computer screen would become real. She would see Layla's motionless form. The only other dead bodies she'd seen had been neatly tucked away in coffins at funerals or displayed scientifically as cadavers when she took an anatomy course.

"You need to stay in the car," Sloan said.

She felt a glimmer of relief. She wasn't squeamish—far from it—but she would rather picture her friend laughing or picking flowers or reading a book. It had taken a long time to partially bury her memories of Layla after her nights as Hardy's "bride." The thought of her death was worse.

Still, Brooke couldn't back down. "If you didn't want my help in your investigation, why did you bring me along?"

"I didn't want you to race up here, half-cocked and looking for trouble."

An unfair characterization if she'd ever heard one. "I'm never half-cocked."

From her fanny pack, she heard the buzz of her

cell phone indicating a text message. While engaged in conversation with another person, she usually ignored texts. But she was worried about Franny.

She checked the message and read it twice: Settle down, Brooke, or you'll be next.

Chapter Four

Sloan took the cell phone from her hand and read the message. The "you'll be next" part seemed like a generic threat, but the effect of the text on Brooke indicated something more significant. Her lower lip quivered. Her blue eyes wavered as though frantically seeking an escape route. For the first time since they'd met, he caught a glimpse of raw vulnerability.

Watching her reaction, he said, "'Settle down,' it says. What's behind those words?"

"Hardy always said that to me. 'Settle down, Brooke.'" Her fingers knotted in her lap, and she stared down at them. "Is the murderer watching us? Is he close enough to see what's going on?"

He couldn't guarantee that she was safe from an observer with binoculars or a rifle scope. This area was too heavily forested, and the hills were dotted with boulders that a sniper could hide behind. "I can arrange for you to be taken home."

"I want to be here. I owe it to Layla." She

hunched her shoulders, fighting her fear. "I can't let a stupid text message throw me."

"A reminder of the past," he suggested.

"I'm fine."

When she looked up, her defenses slammed back into place. She was twice as prickly as before. Her blue eyes were as hard as tempered steel. Her chin jutted at a stubborn angle, and her spine was ramrod stiff. His natural instinct was to be gentle, to reassure her and hold her close, but that wasn't going to happen. If he reached toward her, she might rip his arm off.

The main reason he'd brought her along was to gather information, and he needed to penetrate her shell to find the insights he needed. Keeping his tone conversational, he asked, "When Hardy told you to settle down, what did you do?"

"I settled."

"Did he use that phrase with all of you? Franny mentioned that her mystery caller said something about little ladies who don't behave."

"His commands were different," she said, "depending on our role in the sick, disgusting family he put together."

Sloan waited for her to continue. He'd read about their captivity in Gimbel's reports and knew that Hardy had kidnapped the six young women for different reasons. Only two had been sexually molested: Layla and Sophia. All had been restrained, chained, starved and brutalized.

"His family, ha!" Her rage and loathing erupted. "We weren't allowed to have feelings or opinions. Everything revolved around him. Layla was his bride. Sophia was his girlfriend. The younger girls—Franny and the twins—were his playmates, his little ladies. And if they didn't do as he said, he'd take great pleasure in disciplining them."

Hardy had punished Franny by cutting off the tip of her finger. To make it worse, he'd forced Brooke to hold Franny's wrist and had told her that if she refused, he would lop off the whole hand. Calling them *family* was one of the cruelest things he could do to these foster kids who either had come from dysfunctional families or had been abandoned—or both.

She continued, "I was the mother. My job was to keep the house clean and do the cooking with whatever scraps he brought home. If I dared to ask for more or burned the food or left a speck of dust on the table, he'd tell me to settle down. And there would be a punishment so I wouldn't forget what I'd done wrong."

Her early life had been a horror show, and Sloan was impressed with her fortitude and her ability to handle her post-traumatic stress. Again, he wished he could embrace her. Quietly, he said, "I'm sorry for what you went through."

"Enough about the past," she said abruptly. "We should get on with the investigation."

He'd already decided against bringing her into the cabin crime scene. There was no need to re-traumatize her with the sight of her murdered friend. But how was he going to convince her to stay in the car? Handcuff her to the steering wheel?

"A few more questions," he said. "Tell me about your security at the cabin. Is it like your house? Do you have cameras?"

"Not anymore. I had a couple of motion-sensitive cameras, but they were difficult to maintain. When they got stolen by vandals a few months ago, I never bothered replacing them."

"You had a robbery?"

"An attempted robbery," she said. "There was a screaming loud alarm that went off when someone tried to break in the door. There was nobody close enough to hear it so I got rid of it. All the windows are triple-pane glass, which is really hard to shatter. And there's a dead bolt on the door."

He appreciated her efforts to protect herself and the people she loved. "How often do you come here?"

"At least once a month. Layla is a more frequent visitor." She exhaled an impatient sigh. "Why are you wasting time with these questions?"

"To help me build a profile." He doubted she'd

argue with that logic, but she scoffed. Brooke had never met a nit she didn't pick.

"I don't get it," she muttered. "What do my security precautions tell you about the murderer?"

"The fact that you and Layla kept your cabin locked up tells me that the killer needed to exercise care and intelligence when he chose to use this place. The murder wasn't a random attack. He planned his actions." For the moment, she seemed satisfied. "Now, let's go back to those special phrases, like *settle down*. How many people would know them?"

"Only a few hundred thousand." She gave a cold, ironic laugh. "We were written up in the newspapers and online and in all kinds of journals, plus there was the television documentary by Nick Brancusi."

"He's the same guy who's talking to Sophia in Las Vegas, right?"

"A scum bucket." Anger threaded her voice. "I told Sophia that I'd never agree to another project like the last one, but she was free to do whatever she wanted."

"Sophia is the only one who moved away from the Denver area."

Brooke shrugged. "She always held herself kind of separate, as though she was better than the rest of us, and I'd have to admit that she was definitely the prettiest. After her attempt at a career in Hollywood fizzled, she ended up in

Vegas. She thinks another documentary would be good publicity."

"And you don't."

"Oh, hell no."

He looked through the windshield toward her cabin and saw Gimbel coming down the driveway. The old man gave a cheerful wave. With plastic booties on his feet, his plaid shirt and red suspenders, he looked like a cowboy clown. As soon as Brooke spotted him, she beamed a smile, flung open her car door and dashed toward him. Had she already forgotten the potential watcher in the woods? It didn't seem like her to ignore a threat.

Though she was obviously fond of the retired agent she'd known for twelve years, she was still skittish. First, she shook Gimbel's hand and exchanged hellos, then Gimbel touched her arm and spoke quietly to her, and finally she collapsed against him. It wasn't a real embrace, because Brooke held her stiff arms close to her body, but she allowed the older man to hold her. For a brief moment, her shoulders shuddered, and Sloan thought she might cry. Instead, she tossed her head and stepped back two paces.

"Glad to see you," Sloan said to the former agent. "Would you stay here with Brooke while I take a look inside the cabin?"

"I'm coming with you," Brooke said.

This was where he had to draw the line. "No

civilians at crime scenes. Not until the forensic team is done gathering evidence."

"But it's my house."

"Those are the rules," he said. "But I'm willing to offer a compromise. While I'm inside, I'll take photos. Then I'll bring them out here and show you. If there's anything you have a question about, I can go back in and get an answer. Deal?"

Through clenched teeth, she said, "I don't like it, but okay."

"I've got a problem," Gimbel said. "I'm happy to spend time with Brooke, who's one of my favorite people in the world, but this heat is kicking my tired old butt. Give me your car keys, Sloan. Your FBI-issued SUV has a better cooling system than my truck."

And it provided better protection against watchers. He dropped the keys into Gimbel's waiting hand. "Do you miss the perks of the job?"

"I do, but not the responsibilities."

"Don't worry about us," Brooke said. "We'll stay cool…in your air-conditioning."

A joke? As if she was lighthearted? He did not understand this woman.

Leaving them behind, he strode up the inclined driveway toward the cabin. He hoped to kick-start his profiling before the news of Layla's murder leaked to the media, and he needed to clarify his responsibilities with the other agents involved.

Investigating had already begun. At the edges

of the asphalt driveway, he noticed a few num-bered placards indicating footprints and tire tracks. The one-room log cabin perched on the side of a steep, forested cliff with the front porch facing a retaining wall and a direct view of the opposite side of the canyon. The setting was iso-lated. He doubted there would be witnesses who might have noticed the arrival of the murderer.

At the side door to the cabin, he approached Special Agent Sam Keller, who—like Gimbel—had beaten him to the scene. Disposable booties covered Keller's shoes, indicating that he'd been inside and had chosen to leave. Sloan understood. He hated death scenes. His expertise was discov-ering motive, not dealing with the physical, fo-rensic evidence.

"Hey, Sloan, why did you bring the girl along?" In spite of the circumstances, Keller's greeting was cheerful. "Are you keeping your enemies close? Scared she'll attack you again?"

He never should have mentioned the pepper spray to the other guys in the FBI office. "Have you been inside the cabin?"

"Yeah, and we caught a break. I've arranged for the body to be delivered to our morgue and ME in Denver for autopsy, but the local coroner is a retired MD. He's got preliminary results. Ac-cording to him, she's been dead for over forty-eight hours."

Brooke would be relieved to know that Layla

had been killed before yesterday when she checked the camera in the cabin. Nothing could have been done to prevent her friend's murder. "Cause of death?"

"Ligature strangulation. No defensive wounds." Keller lowered his sunglasses and glared over the rims. "Assistant Director Martinez put me in charge of this investigation. Everything coordinates through me."

His alpha-male stance was unnecessary, because Sloan didn't want to be the boss. "It makes sense for you to take the lead. I haven't been here long and don't have your connections with the locals. There could be jurisdictional problems."

"Count on it." He pushed his glasses back onto the bridge of his nose and leaned back on his heels to make himself look taller. "Anything that involves the Hardy Dolls is high profile."

He had the distinct feeling that Keller enjoyed the attention. "I suppose you'll be talking to the media."

"I've got no choice. They're going to want a statement." He preened. "I'll keep the murder quiet for as long as possible, but things are going to get crazy. I wasn't at the Denver office twelve years ago, but I saw the segments on national TV news shows."

Sloan remembered the sad photos of six little girls. "It was a lot of coverage."

"Have you ever been part of a big story like that?"

During his years in Texas, he'd participated in several serial killer investigations but had never been the agent in charge. "Here's what I'm thinking, Keller. I'd like to spend most of my time with Brooke and the other women, setting up profiles and following leads. I'll report directly to you."

"Fair enough."

In the interest of full cooperation, he told Keller about the text Brooke had received and suggested they might want to search the hillsides. Quick and efficient, Keller dispatched a couple of the local law enforcement officers who were hanging around outside the cabin, waiting for the FBI forensic people.

He glanced over at Sloan. "The coroner's still inside, if you want to talk to him."

Before entering through the side door, Sloan put on booties and latex gloves. "Were there signs of a break-in?"

"No scratches on the wood frame. No pry marks. Both doors—the one in front and this one—were unlocked when the locals arrived."

"What about a vehicle? Was her car here?"

"No car," Keller said. "The killer must have transported her to the cabin in his vehicle and then left."

A preliminary picture formed in Sloan's mind. Two days ago, Layla had been murdered somewhere else. Today, between eleven thirty and two, when Brooke checked the camera, the killer brought her here. Why did he wait two days? Why here? Why go to the trouble of bringing her to the mountains?

Bracing himself for what he'd see inside, he entered through the side door. The interior of the one-room cabin was paneled in warm, knotty pine. Waist-high shelving units separated the kitchen and dining table from the bedroom and desk area. The A-frame ceiling and open beams made the area seem larger than the actual square footage.

Sloan didn't need to look at the bed to know that death was close. Some people claimed that the smell of death was sweet. Sloan had never thought so. The stink tainted the air and welcomed the ubiquitous buzzing flies.

A spry gray-haired gentleman came toward him, introduced himself as the coroner and shook hands. "The name is Edwards, but everybody calls me Dr. Ted."

"I'm SA Justin Sloan, FBI. Did you know the deceased?"

"I only met her and her friend one time at a community meeting to discuss the beaver problem. With their matching black hair and blue eyes, they were striking women. I recalled the story of their kidnapping but didn't mention it to anyone else. I don't much care for gossip." His frown emphasized his long, horsey-looking face. "It was a real shame what happened to those young girls. And now this?"

Sloan saw a flicker of empathy in Dr. Ted's eyes, but he didn't fit the stereotype of a kindly small-town doctor. He was cool and methodical. Murder didn't shock him. "How long have you been in practice in the mountains?"

"After I retired from the VA hospital, I moved up here and started a small general practice. That was about eight years ago. I still see a couple of patients now and then."

"And you're also the coroner," Sloan said. "What can you tell me in addition to time of death and probable cause?"

"I'm guessing that when your ME does an autopsy and runs a tox screen, he'll find trace amounts of sedative or narcotic in her system. She must have been drugged. Otherwise she would have put up some kind of fight."

There were other explanations for the lack of defensive wounds. "She might have been purposely nonresistant in an attempt to outsmart her killer."

"Not likely," the doctor said. "Even if she was trying to be cagey, her instinct would be to struggle."

Thinking of what Brooke had told him about their captivity and Layla's role as Hardy's "wife," he asked, "Was she raped?"

"No external trauma to the genitals, but you'll need a rape kit to know for sure."

"Can you tell if she was tied up or restrained?"

"I didn't find marks on her wrists or ankles." He went to the bedside and stood looking down thoughtfully at the dead woman, who was covered to her chin by a flowered peach comforter. "No unusual bruising."

"You rearranged the body."

"How did you know that?"

Sloan thought twice before speaking. He never liked to give out more information than necessary. "Before we drove up here, Brooke and I saw her on a computer feed."

"Agent Keller took photos of the way we found her. He asked me not to take off her nightgown, but I pulled back the covers to get a better look."

Gazing down at Layla's face differed from viewing her image on a computer screen. Her cheeks and eye sockets were hollow, and her skin had taken on a grayish pallor. The only color came from the Rosy Posey lipstick. Sloan was glad he could spare Brooke from seeing this tragic end to her friend's life.

"There isn't any blood," he said.

"I didn't notice any external lacerations, but there might have been superficial scratches. She was carefully scrubbed, probably postmortem." The doctor leaned over the body and took a whiff.

"You can smell bleach. Her hair was washed and combed out, nice and pretty."

With his gloved hand, Sloan adjusted the position of the body. "The side of her left arm is discolored."

"Also her left shoulder and the left side of her back. I figure that shortly after she was murdered, she was positioned in such a way that she was lying on her side, maybe curled up in the trunk of a car. The blood drained to the lowest point."

Wishing he could be more detached, Sloan avoided thinking of this husk as a vibrant young woman with her future ahead of her. Instead, he stuck to direct observations. "She couldn't have been in the trunk of a car for long, not in this heat."

"You're right about that. Her body was kept in a cool place, like a cellar or somewhere air-conditioned. Otherwise, decomp would be further along, and we'd have maggots."

Not something he wanted to think about. "Any jewelry other than the wedding band?"

"Not a thing," the doctor said. "She didn't dress herself. Panties were on backward."

From a profiling standpoint, the act of redressing her was significant. The killer had also washed and combed her hair. Her body had been arranged in an almost respectful pose—fully dressed with her hands folded below her breasts. Her killer cared about her and didn't want to humiliate her. The wedding ring and the lipstick indicated a familiarity with Layla's past.

"Thanks, Dr. Ted. I appreciate your expert help."

"I hope you catch the son of a bitch who did this."

"So do I."

In the kitchen, Sloan recognized Brooke's touch in the neatly arranged shelves and drawers. Other than canned goods, there wasn't much in the way of food. The fridge held a jar of pickles along with mustard and other condiments. The contents were unremarkable, but he took several photos for Brooke.

Likewise, he snapped pictures of the shelves. A bridal magazine on the desk seemed out of place. The forensic team would take fingerprints, but he doubted they'd be lucky enough to find anything useful. He checked out the tiny lens tucked away in a crystal vase on a shelf opposite the bed. Too bad the camera hadn't been set up for constant surveillance.

Outside, he inhaled a deep breath. He stretched and shook himself, knowing that the smell of death would cling to him for hours.

Keller approached. "It makes sense for you to contact the other women."

"Got it," Sloan said. "When Brooke and I get back to town, I want to check out Layla's apartment."

"With Brooke tagging along?"

"She could be helpful. She knows every detail of their time in captivity, and she was particularly close to Layla. Brooke might come up with insights that I wouldn't notice."

"Is that so?" Keller was openly skeptical.

"You bet." *Profiler, heal thyself.* His rationale for taking her along wasn't great. Sloan acknowledged to himself that he wanted to spend more time with Brooke because he liked being with her. For Keller's benefit, he gave other excuses. "She's smart. For example, she's been checking the camera in the cabin and discovered a window of time—between eleven thirty this morning and two this afternoon—when the killer must have brought Layla's body here."

"Okay," Keller said. "I'll keep the timing in mind when we interview witnesses and check surveillance cameras on the highway."

"I'll be in touch," Sloan said.

He saw Brooke storming up the driveway with Agent Gimbel in her wake. Her former vulnerability was gone. Her eyes flashed blue flames. She looked like Joan of Arc, ready for battle as she stomped toward him, holding her cell phone aloft.

Oh, yeah, she was going to be a great help.

Chapter Five

Never a patient woman, Brooke held herself to a high standard and expected the same from everybody else. Sloan had taken too long to explore a one-room cabin, and she'd just received a text message from Tom Lancaster, the attorney who handled her and the other five. Mentally she corrected herself—there were only four. Layla was gone.

Her absence echoed in Brooke's mind, distracting her and pulling her toward sadness. She would miss her friend. They'd been as close as sisters, maybe even closer. The time for mourning would come later. Right now she needed to find the killer and end this threat before anyone else was hurt.

She came to a halt in front of Sloan. "Is it safe for me to be out here?"

"I can't guarantee anything," he said, "but several deputies and cops are scouring the hillsides, looking for the person who sent the threatening text."

She scanned the forested hills and spotted a uniformed officer. "It doesn't seem likely that this murderer is a sniper."

"You're right. Killing from afar doesn't fit the profile."

"Does that mean you have a profile?"

"The start of one," he said.

She needed to know more about the current status of the investigation and what she should tell Lancaster, but she held herself in check and lowered her phone. He introduced her to Agent Keller, a deputy and the local doctor she'd met before and refused to call "Dr. Ted" because it made her think of the long-ago television show about Mr. Ed, the talking horse.

Forcing herself to stay calm, she pulled Sloan to one side. "We need to hurry. I just got a text from our attorney."

"Is that why you were frantically waving that phone at me?"

She didn't acknowledge his implication that she was overly excited. "Lancaster has been trying to reach Layla. Should I tell him about the murder or not? Should I lie to him? What do I say?"

"Don't call him back."

His simple solution didn't cover all the bases. "If Lancaster is looking for her, there might be other people she has appointments with. How do I handle them?"

"That's not really what's bothering you, is it?"

He was too perceptive. *Annoying.* "It's the media," she said darkly.

"You don't want reporters to ask questions before you're prepared."

"I don't want them anywhere near me or my friends."

"I understand," he said. "It's important for us to get ahead of the media. Franny shouldn't have to hear about her friend's death on the five o'clock news."

"She'd be heartbroken." To be honest, Brooke was close to having her own panic attack, and she had a hundred times more self-control than Franny and the twins. She unzipped her fanny pack and tucked the phone inside. "Let's get this over with. I need to go inside the cabin."

"I can't let you do that. Not until after the forensic crew is done."

"But this is my property." Her well-practiced assertive voice masked her sense of relief. She ought to be able to investigate like a pro, but she dreaded what she would see. The image of Layla on the computer had been horrible. Still, she said, "If I want to go inside, I can."

"I advise against it."

"But you can't stop me," she said.

"Actually, I can. This is a crime scene."

They were at a standoff. She didn't want to argue with him…or maybe she did. Maybe she needed to fight, to be angry and build a barrier between them so she wouldn't collapse against his shoulder and weep.

"Excuse me." Agent Gimbel hitched up his baggy jeans and inserted himself into their conversation. "Here's a thought, Brooke. Why don't you stay here with Sloan, and I'll go to your house in Denver and keep an eye on Franny?"

"I should be the one who tells her about Layla," she said.

"Agreed," Gimbel said. "And I won't tell her. I'll stay at her side and keep her away from the news. Won't say a word until you're there."

"She shouldn't be alone."

"I can handle this," Gimbel said. "Trust me."

She turned her back on Gimbel and Sloan. *How can I trust them?* They couldn't possibly understand what her life was like. They hadn't walked a mile in her shoes. They didn't see Franny the way she did—as a ten-year-old child, broken and tortured. How could anyone else be trusted to do the right thing? "I'm not sure."

Gimbel said, "Trust is one of the issues you've worked on with your therapist."

"It is," she admitted. And she was overdue for an appointment with Dr. Joan. Until yesterday, her life had seemed to be on track. "Give me a minute to think."

Her options were simple: hitch a ride back to town with Agent Gimbel, talk to Franny and contact the twins, or stay here with Sloan and dig into the investigation. She remembered the text message warning that she would be the next to go. Her priority should be to discover the identity of the killer so they'd all be safe.

She whipped around to face the two men. "Thank you, Agent Gimbel. I appreciate your offer to take care of Franny. If you need me, you have my cell number."

After he smiled and patted her on the shoulder, he ambled down the driveway to where his truck was parked. When she turned and met Sloan's gaze, she noticed an assessing look in his eye that made her feel like a bug under a microscope, waiting to be dissected. She didn't want to be analyzed.

"If you won't let me go through the cabin," she said, "why am I here?"

"Good question, and I'll try to give you a reasonable answer. You're not a trained investigator, but you're smart and I trust your insights. If Layla's murder is related to the threats you've all been receiving, I think you'll be able to make those connections a lot quicker than I could."

"Even though you're an ace profiler."

"Even though," he said. "First, I want to be sure the murder is related to what happened twelve years ago."

She threw her hands in the air. "What else could it be?"

"Layla had a life that was unconnected to her early trauma."

Not really. How could she explain to him? A life-shattering experience touched every part of you and never faded. Like a broken vase that had been superglued back together, the trauma was always evident. The victim was always fragile, easily broken. "You mentioned that you took pictures inside the cabin?"

Taking his phone from his pocket, he scrolled through the photos. "I'm guessing that you aren't impressed with my psychological skills. You probably don't think I can understand you."

"Maybe."

"Give me a chance," he said. "I want to know what's going on inside you."

When she thought of tall, gorgeous Agent Sloan being inside her, Brooke tried not to take him literally. A giggle escaped her lips. *Hysterical laughter?* She was tempted to make a very silly and inappropriate joke about how she might be open to his probing analysis.

Glancing over her shoulder, she saw a van park at the end of the driveway. A four-man crew climbed out. Two of them wore FBI T-shirts and caps. "The forensic guys?"

"They got here quicker than I expected. Still, it'll take a couple of hours for them to process the evidence."

And she'd have to wait, to sit idly by while her

anxiety built to an unbearable level. "I can't stand it. Let's take a look at those photos."

She led him down the driveway to a picnic table that had been positioned to catch the afternoon sunlight slicing through the trees. Side by side, they sat on the attached bench and watched the forensic team approach her cabin, pausing at the side door to put on booties and gloves. "What are they going to do? Take fingerprints and look for fibers and stuff?"

"Something like that," he said. "This is a nice little cabin. Tell me about how you and Layla decided to buy it."

"The property belonged to one of the doctors I do transcriptions for, and he sold it for a great price. We were both feeling stressed—Layla and me—and we thought it might be good to have a place where we could escape and unwind."

Growing up as a foster kid, she'd never had a family home, and she'd thoroughly enjoyed the process of furnishing and redesigning her house in Denver to suit her needs. When she heard about the deal she could get on this cabin, Brooke saw another opportunity to create a special sanctuary. She and Layla had talked about adding another room or building a garage. She used to feel safe here.

She gazed past the yellow crime-scene tape to the window beside the door, where sunlight glinted on the triple-pane glass they'd had installed for insulation and protection. They'd done most of the work on the cabin themselves. On a long weekend, they'd painted the window frames green to match the door and the railing on the front porch. "I always wished we had a fireplace. We were planning to install a potbelly stove."

"Have you done a lot of work here?"

"I like do-it-yourself projects. They're a hobby." She smiled at the thought of Layla installing the bathroom faucets backward with the hot on the cold water and vice versa. "I have good memories."

"That's what you want to hang on to."

He was right. She didn't want to go inside and face the horrible reality of death. Instead, Brooke would remember Layla trying to paint the window frames without getting a single smear on her shirt. "We used to come out to this picnic table in the afternoon and drink lemonade."

He held up a photo of the nearly empty fridge. "I'm guessing that you didn't keep the refrigerator stocked."

"Not unless we knew we were going to be here for more than a day or two." She scowled at the photo. "Layla didn't bring any food. She didn't intend to stay."

"It's doubtful that she planned to come here at all," he said. "According to Dr. Ted, she's been dead for over forty-eight hours."

The time of death information hit her like a bolt of electricity. "Since Wednesday?"

"More or less. The autopsy will give us more accurate information."

She was relieved. There was nothing she could have done to keep Layla safe. The murderer had struck before Brooke was aware of the threat. "That means she probably wasn't killed here at the cabin."

"I doubt that this is the primary crime scene. I expect the forensic team to confirm that."

She looked at the cabin with fresh eyes. If she could insulate herself with good memories, she might be able to reclaim this sanctuary, to live here and make the improvements that she and Layla had talked about. She wouldn't be haunted by the ghost of a murderer. "How was she killed?"

To her surprise, Sloan set down his phone on the picnic table and grasped her hand. His touch warmed her. When his gaze linked with hers, the official FBI agent morphed into a different person. In his multifaceted gray eyes, she saw sympathy, kindness and a sharp edge of curiosity that kept him from being a sentimental goop. The bustle and activity around them faded to background noise as he asked, "How much do you want to know?"

"All of it. If I'm going to be any help to you, I need details."

"We'll have to wait for the official autopsy for

complete information, but I trust Dr. Ted's findings. He believes she died from ligature asphyxiation. That means—"

"I know what it means." She yanked her hand away from him. "You don't need to be condescending with me. My job is to input transcriptions for doctors, and I understand the terminology. You're saying that Layla was strangled with a cord or a chain."

"There were no bruises or lacerations that showed she'd been restrained," he said. "The lack of defensive wounds indicates that she didn't struggle."

"Was she drugged?"

"That would be my guess, but we won't know for sure until after the autopsy and tox screen."

She hoped Layla had been unconscious and hadn't felt any pain when the ligature tightened around her throat and cut off her air. Through pinched lips, she forced out the single word that encapsulated Layla's worst fear. "Raped?"

"We won't know until there's a rape kit." He leaned forward on the bench so he could see her face. "Do you want to hear more?"

Not really. Her heart was beating too fast, and her lungs constricted. But she couldn't stop now. She had to get past her fears if she meant to find the killer. When she stood, her balance shifted. The afternoon heat hammered down upon her. Her face flushed. A rivulet of sweat trickled between her breasts. "What did she look like, in person?"

He stood beside her, a steadying presence. "She was posed under the covers with her hands folded."

"When you say 'posed,' what does that mean?"

"Neatly dressed in a nightgown, she'd been scrubbed clean. Her hair was washed. Her features were calm."

Brooke wanted to believe that death had come gently to Layla, and she was finally at peace. *It still wasn't right.* "Can you arrange protection for the twins and for Sophia in Vegas?"

"I'll talk to Agent Keller."

She knew better than to expect guarantees of safety from the local police and the FBI. They didn't have the manpower to act as bodyguards. The only way she could keep all of them safe was to hire a private security firm. "Let me see more of those pictures."

He scrolled through the photos he'd taken of the wall opposite the bed. In the bathroom, he'd opened the medicine cabinet. When he returned to pictures of the kitchen, she finally noticed something significant. She pointed to the screen. "There it is."

"Could you be more specific?"

"You wanted proof that Layla's murder was connected to Martin Hardy? It's right there." She shuddered. "Do you see the apron hanging on a hook in the kitchen?"

"What about it?"

"Blue gingham," she said. "It's a message for me."

"Why?"

Every day of her captivity, she'd worn an apron that looked exactly like the one in the photo. When she spilled on it or when it had been stained with blood, she'd scrubbed and scrubbed it in the sink until the gingham was spotless and bright. Hardy wouldn't stand for her to be messy. His little mama had to be perfectly clean.

"I don't think the pattern of the apron was mentioned in the reports," she said.

Never would she forget that pale shade of blue and the innocent checkerboard pattern. Her nightmares were filled with images of being strangled by that apron. The ties took on a life of their own as they tightened around her throat and cut off her air. Ligature asphyxiation, just like Layla.

Chapter Six

During the drive into town, Brooke buried her fears and sorrow while she figured out what to do next. In the driver's seat beside her, Sloan talked to his colleagues on his hands-free phone. His conversations were quick and cryptic. No more Mr. Nice Guy Profiler, he was all business, all cop. She found his lawman persona sexy—a distraction she didn't want right now.

Looking down into her lap, she considered her first order of business: Make sure everyone had adequate protection. Franny would continue to stay with her. The twins were more problematic. One of them, Megan, had managed to create a normal life with a husband and child in the suburbs. Somehow, she had to convince the whole family to accept protection. The other twin, Moira, was an artist and more footloose. Then there was Sophia in Las Vegas, who would need her own bodyguard.

Next on her list of things to do was making contact with Tom Lancaster. Not only would he be useful in handling the arrangements associated with Layla's murder, but he could also administer her will. If they needed to hire bodyguards for an extended period of time, Tom had access to their joint funds and investments.

With the sun setting behind them, the SUV crested a hill, and she looked down on the silhouette of downtown Denver. The red glow from the skies reflected off distant skyscrapers while a stream of taillights marked the route into the city.

"This view makes me think of Oz," Sloan said. "I like the way the tall buildings rise from the plains."

"After you've been here for a while, you won't think it's such a magical place."

"Why not?"

"For one thing, magic doesn't exist. Life isn't a fairy tale." At least, not *her* life. She couldn't waste time believing in ogres, witches and ghouls when a real-life monster had murdered her best friend. "Also, the traffic is awful and the whole city is under construction with new apartments springing up like mushrooms. It's getting crowded here. Don't get me wrong, Denver is a great place to live. The weather is sunny. It's relatively clean with plenty of parks, museums and galleries."

"And weed," he said.

"Not my thing, but I appreciate the systematic

approach the state has taken to the implementation of the marijuana trade."

"Ditto."

She checked her precision wristwatch. It had been twenty-seven minutes since they left the cabin, longer than that since Gimbel joined Franny at her house. He'd called her once with an update. "As soon as we're done at Layla's apartment, we need to get back to my house. Gimbel has things under control. The twins are coming over to my house, and Franny is getting suspicious, especially since there's a protective police car parked in front of the house—which, by the way, I appreciate."

"You're welcome."

She was duly impressed that law enforcement was operating efficiently. From what she'd overheard of his conversations on the phone, she could tell that the pieces were shifting into place. "How can I help move the investigation forward?"

"It's hard to believe that Martin Hardy had friends, but there were a few. Also, there were witnesses and relatives—people who knew enough about what happened to threaten you."

"With things like the wedding band, the lipstick and that horrible gingham apron."

"What can you tell me about those people? Do you remember them?"

"I remember everything."

Even though she hated her dark thoughts of

the past, she recalled a face at the window in
the moonlight. Black hair, full beard, sunken
cheeks and a nose as thin as a knife blade, he had
watched her as she slept with her right wrist and
ankle cuffed to the bedframe. With her free hand,
she had signaled to him and she had whispered,
"Help me." Hoping that she'd finally found someone who would set them free, she twisted around
and repeated, "Help me, help me, help me." His
deep-set eyes had been invisible in their dark
sockets, but she could tell that he was grinning.

He had returned several times to torment her.
"Zachary Doyle, the bastard."

"A peeping Tom," Sloan said. "He lived less
than a mile away from the cabin where you were
held. You identified him from mug shots."

"At the time I knew his face but not his name."
She'd never confronted him. None of Martin Hardy's possible accomplices had been allowed in the
courtroom during the trial. Her testimony had
been taped in the judge's chambers.

"You never forgot him."

"He's kind of a recurring nightmare," she said.
"Are we going to question him?"

"Maybe. I'll arrange for an officer to stop by
his house and check his alibi. Is there anybody
else you remember?"

"There was a brother-in-law. I never actually
saw him, but his son came to the cabin to play
with the younger girls. The kid claimed to be

eleven but looked younger." He must be twenty-three or twenty-four by now, a grown man. "His name was Peter Channing. Martin enjoyed when the boy was there. Peter completed his fantasy of creating a family."

"Any others?"

"Not that I knew. Six or seven times, Martin brought friends to the cabin. They had sex with Layla and Sophia while the girls were blindfolded. None of those scumbags were identified." She could only hope there was a special place in hell reserved for them. She shuddered. "Do you think those guys worried that Layla might see them on the street and recognize them?"

"It's a motive for murder."

"True, but I don't believe it." She unzipped her fanny pack and took out a packet of tissues that she used to blow her nose. The conversation was making her fidget. "If Layla had seen them, she would have told me. She's a lawyer now. She'd find a legal way to make them pay."

They rode in silence while dusk spread across the mountains and plains. The shadowy landscape seemed appropriate for the haze of memory that lurked at the edge of her conscious thoughts. If she closed her eyes, she could see Doyle. Never would she forget the whimpers from the bedroom when Hardy brought his so-called friends to the cabin.

"At the start of an investigation," he said,

"there's one question that needs an answer. Why now? What triggered the attack on Layla? This wasn't an impulsive murder. The killer planned ahead to drug her."

Picking apart the pieces of the crime didn't disturb her. In fact, it was the opposite, somewhat soothing. She liked to apply logic to what was intrinsically a senseless act. "Layla must have become a threat to the killer, but I don't know why. She was graduating from law school and preparing to set up a practice."

"Did she mention anything about Peter Channing, Doyle or anyone else connected with Hardy?"

"She didn't say anything to me." Brooke made a mental note. "I'll talk to the others."

"It's possible that the murderer wasn't directly a part of the long-ago crime. He could be part of that vast, faceless mass of lawbreakers and perverts who were aroused by the highly publicized stories of your captivity."

"Copycats," she said with disgust, "creeps who want to be like Hardy."

"With one big difference," he said. "Hardy never killed anyone. Layla's murder means this copycat has taken his obsession to a different level."

"How will you narrow the crowd?" she asked.

"A combination of police work and profiling. When I interview each of you, certain names will rise to the surface. I'll check the names against criminal records, and the threat will become clearer."

Her contacts with the outside world were few and far between. Most of her transcription work was done online with no physical meetings. "I won't have much to tell you."

"Don't be so sure," he said. "Over the course of the past month, you might have had workers to the house. And you go out into the world to shop, to get gas for your SUV, to pick up dinner. Maybe you go to church."

"Not lately, but I get your point. No man—or woman—is an island."

Following the GPS directions, he exited the highway and drove north on Lincoln toward downtown. Layla's apartment was located in the Capitol Hill area amid a cluster of other high-rise buildings. The front entry required a key, but they wouldn't need to bother the concierge. Brooke had both of her friend's keys for use in emergencies.

Outside Layla's apartment building, Sloan parked the SUV at the curb. "As of right now, I'm your bodyguard. I exit the car before you, scan the area and open your door."

His authoritative tone made her blink. "Okay, if you say so."

"You sound surprised."

"Usually, I'm the one giving orders. I take care of everybody else."

"It's my turn now."

He escorted her to the entry, where she used her key to open the door. The open counter in front of the office was vacant, and she led the way across the furnished lobby to the elevators. Layla's apartment was on the seventh floor.

"Before we leave, I'll talk to the concierge," he said as he stepped onto the elevator. "I should let her know that the forensic team will be dropping by. And I want to take a look at the tapes from their surveillance cameras."

She'd checked out the security with Layla before she moved here. There were cameras at every entrance and in the underground parking garage. Each apartment had a dead-bolt lock. Brooke hoped it had been enough. A shudder trickled down her spine. She didn't want to walk into the apartment and find a pool of blood staining the beige carpet. "Do you think she was killed here?"

"If we see any signs of violence, we'll leave and let the CSIs do their work."

Mentally preparing herself for the worst, she turned the key in the lock and stepped aside to let him go first. She followed him into a small, square entryway that led to a hallway. Something was wrong! Carefully, she went down the hall to the front room with the forest green sectional and the glass-topped coffee table.

"Oh, no, this is horrible."

The killer had been here. He had violated Layla's home.

SLOAN HAD NO idea why Brooke was so upset. She gasped and came to an abrupt halt in the front room. Her entire body went tense, and she looked like she was in shock.

He saw nothing disturbing. Layla's apartment was tidy and pleasant with modern furniture and a balcony view of the mountains. To the right was a long trestle dining table with a couple of stinky candles and a cactus garden as a centerpiece.

Brooke jolted into action. She unzipped her fanny pack and took out a pair of purple latex gloves. She passed another pair to him. "We should wear these. I'm sure there are prints all over the apartment."

He wasn't sure what bothered him the most: the fact that she carried latex gloves in her fanny pack or his negligence. He hadn't expected her apartment to be a potential crime scene. "If there's really a problem, we need to step aside and let forensics come through here first."

"I'll be careful." In a nervous frenzy, she darted from the coffee table to the dining room table. "I mean, the place is trashed."

Giving her plenty of room, he stepped back and observed. Brooke's intimate knowledge of Layla might uncover more evidence than an expert FBI team of CSI investigators. She pointed to a stack of books beside an overstuffed chair. "Look at this Leaning Tower of Pisa. Layla would never put hardbacks on top of paperbacks. And the trash can is half-filled with envelopes and receipts."

"Why is that unusual?" he asked.

"She shreds the paperwork to guard against identity theft."

Okay, that wasn't so weird. Lots of people were careful with their trash. "What else?"

"You can tell by the marks on the carpet that this standing lamp has been moved. And the sliding door on the credenza is open."

He squinted at the credenza. "That gap can't be more than two inches wide."

"Layla would never leave it like that. It's obvious that somebody went through her things, searching for something." She bent double to study the gap. "Is it all right if I pull this door open, or should I wait for the forensic people?"

"Let me take a picture." He aimed the camera in his phone. "You can open it but don't go through the stuff inside."

"The books on the lower shelf are out of order," she said.

How the hell could she tell? "What makes you think so?"

"The spines are out of alignment. I'm guessing that an intruder took them out one by one and searched through the pages."

If so, the so-called intruder had to be the most OCD searcher in the history of modern crime. "Can you tell if anything is missing?"

"I don't know." She straightened and braced her fists on her hips above the strap for the fanny pack. She looked youthful with her black hair pulled up in a loose ponytail and her casual blouse and shorts. But her determination gave her a sense of gravity. Slowly, she shook her head. "I can't be sure if the intruder found what he was looking for."

In the bedroom, she noticed that the lid on the jewelry box was up, organization in the closet was disturbed and the drawers in the dresser weren't closed all the way. These tiny details might be clues, but they could just as likely be coincidence. Though Layla was as compulsively neat as Brooke, an open lid on a jewelry box didn't prove anything.

The second bedroom was a home office, where—once again—Brooke found several bits of disorder. She sat at the light green acrylic desk with drawers on each side. "Is it all right if I check out her computer?"

He snapped a couple of photos of the desk. In his capacity as a federal agent, Sloan knew that he should back off and save the computer research for the FBI cybercrime investigators. But the main reason he'd brought Brooke along was for her unique insights into Layla and the murder. "Do you know her password?"

"It's OCD321, a combination of her diagnosis and her birthday—March 21." She opened the lid on the laptop. "Can I?"

"Don't delete or change anything." He doubted they'd find much. If there had been evidence, the intruder would simply have stolen the computer. "What about a thumb drive or some other kind of data storage?"

"Right here." She opened the top right drawer and pointed to a padded case the size of a deck of cards. Inside were slots for thumb drives. He couldn't tell at a glance if anything had been removed. Again, if the intruder wanted to hide evidence, he would have grabbed the case.

He watched as Brooke brought up the geometric-patterned screen saver and checked out the files and apps. Without asking his permission, she opened the email and started scrolling down the list of messages and ads. Her speed and quick comprehension impressed him, but he wasn't surprised. Her job required excellent computer skills.

Prowling through the office, he began to develop a sense of Layla's identity. Like Brooke, she kept her world under control with strict efficiency, but she didn't seem to be cold or unfeeling. The photographs and keepsakes in her office were polished and dusted, lovingly tended. He circled the desk to the left side, where the drawers appeared to be locked. As he reached down to try the bottom drawer, Brooke spoke up.

"Look at this file. The label says 'PChanning.'"

"Peter Channing."

The first email in the file was dated two weeks ago. It said, Been thinking of you, Layla. I'd like to meet.

Though Layla hadn't responded, Peter had sent four messages. The final one was dated a week ago and was longer than the others.

"I don't believe it," Brooke said. "He says he's getting married."

The impending wedding might be the trigger for Channing to confront his past. "What's the date for the wedding?"

"He doesn't say. I need to make a note of this and of his email." She pulled open the left-side drawer of Layla's desk, looking for a scrap of paper. "Oh my God!"

Inside, he saw a tangle of wires. A bomb. The digital countdown showed less than four minutes.

Chapter Seven

The red digital numbers on the device tucked inside the desk drawer silently counted down. Brooke stared as the clock went from 3:48 to 3:47 and then 3:46. In three minutes and forty-six seconds, the bomb would explode.

Sloan grabbed her arm and yanked her out of the desk chair with such force that her knees buckled. Roughly, he dragged her upright and shoved her toward the door leading from Layla's home office. "Go," he commanded. "Go. Now."

"Can you make it stop?"

Instead of answering, he propelled her toward the exit. This wasn't right. *A bomb?* Layla's possessions would be destroyed. Brooke dashed from the office, past the trestle table, the credenza, the sofa and tasteful chairs. All this would be gone. The evidence would be wiped out.

In the corridor outside the apartment, Sloan hit the fire alarm. A siren wailed through the hallway. Lights above the alarm flashed, strobe-like. He pushed her toward one of the apartments next to Layla's. "Knock on the door. Get everybody out."

He went to the neighboring apartment on the other side. With a heavy fist, he hammered on the door and shouted, "Emergency. There's a bomb."

A young woman holding a yappy little dog peeked into the hallway.

"Get out," Sloan yelled over the screeching fire alarm. "Take the staircase. Go."

Brooke relayed the same message to the young couple in the apartment where she was knocking. The man gave her a curious look and said, "Layla, is that you?"

People often confused them because of their matching black hair and blue eyes. His mistake touched a nerve. Losing Layla was like losing her sister, her twin, a piece of herself that meant she'd never be whole again. Layla was gone. Evidence of her killer would soon be destroyed. She couldn't think about that now. "Just go. Save yourself."

Other doors on the seventh floor swung open. Sloan waved the residents toward the stairwell. *Don't use the elevator in case of fire or electrical emergency.* She clearly remembered the safety precaution rules. Though scared, this fear was different from when she was a helpless child. A bomb threat was more like combat. She wasn't out of control. Neither was Sloan. He directed the evacuation with one hand and made phone calls with the other. He never lost his cool. Was he contacting the fire department, or did the FBI have a special team for dealing with explosive devices?

The apartment corridor was almost empty. It was time for her and Sloan to follow the others. The red digital numbers on the clock must be close to zero.

He held her arm as he opened the door to the concrete stairwell. Other residents from other floors of the high-rise were already on the stairs. It was crowded, but everyone moved in an orderly fashion while grumbling and complaining about the inconvenience. They didn't yet know that the bomb was real.

"Stay close," Sloan whispered in her ear. "The stairwell is dangerous."

"Why?"

"The person who killed Layla is still at large."

She hadn't forgotten.

The metal door from the seventh floor was almost closed when she caught a glimpse of raging orange flames and heard the explosion, crashing and echoing. Loud. Violent. Terrible. The floor shuddered beneath her feet. The building seemed to sway.

Voices in the stairwell changed from conversation to sobs and screams. They were yelling. Chaos rippled through the crowd. If Sloan hadn't been at her side with his arm around her waist, she might have lost it.

He was good in a crisis. He instructed people to move carefully and get out onto the street. He assured them that the fire department was on the way.

The lights in the stairwell blinked out. A smothering blackness enveloped them. In the dark, every voice sounded like a threat. Every accidental nudge felt like someone grabbing at her, slipping a knife between her ribs, poking the barrel of a gun against her skull. Disoriented, she forced herself to move forward, clinging to the railing. Sloan and others held up their cell phones, providing light.

Only seven stories, but she felt like she'd been trapped in the stairwell for hours. When she burst into the lobby with the others, Brooke almost wept with relief. Still staying close to Sloan, she allowed herself to be herded out the front door.

A fire truck roared up to the entrance of the building. Two police cars were already parked at the curb, and she could hear the siren from an ambulance. As soon as the emergency people emerged from their vehicles, they stared up at the seventh floor. She looked over her shoulder and saw flames and gushing black smoke.

"Keep moving," Sloan said. He guided her along the sidewalk with an iron grip on her arm. "I need to get you away from here."

"It's okay. I'll be fine."

"I've done a crap job of protecting you, Brooke. Let me make it right."

Her instinct was to assert herself, but she wasn't a fool. If a trained agent like Sloan thought she needed protecting, she should pay attention and follow his instructions. She noticed that he'd drawn his gun and wished that she'd insisted on bringing her own weapon. The pepper spray in her fanny pack felt woefully inadequate.

While Sloan identified himself to a uniformed officer and asked for assistance, she unzipped her fanny pack and reached inside. Sloan might feel better about the supposedly "crap job" he'd done if he knew that she'd slipped the storage case with Layla's thumb drives into her pack. At the time she took the data, she'd thought she might be tampering with evidence. Now, she congratulated herself on her foresight. The bomb hadn't destroyed everything.

A FEW HOURS AFTER he sent Brooke home with a police officer, Sloan returned to her house. He parked his SUV at the curb opposite her tidy, well-protected abode. The two-story white stucco glistened in the moonlight like a fairy-tale castle. Instead of a dragon and a moat, a cop car with an officer behind the wheel was parked in front. There were other vehicles on the street, and George Gimbel's truck was in the driveway outside the attached garage.

The old man had agreed to stay with Franny until Sloan came back from FBI headquarters. Gimbel hadn't taken much convincing. Sloan had the impression that the retired agent enjoyed his advisory role in the investigation. He obviously liked these six women and felt protective toward them. Twelve years ago, their abduction had been his case. Partly due to his efforts, their captor had been tried, convicted and sentenced to life in prison. Right now, when danger had resurfaced, Gimbel didn't want them to be hurt again.

Sloan exited his air-conditioned car, straightened his necktie and fastened one button on his navy blue blazer. If he'd still been in Texas, the August temperatures would have been uncomfortable. But this was Colorado, where the nights were cooler. During the three months he'd lived in Denver, people had told him repeatedly that it was a dry heat.

Nonetheless, he was sweating. The bomb at Layla's apartment had shaken his confidence and made him plenty angry. On the plus side, the fire department had extinguished the blaze quickly, and nobody had been seriously injured. But those two details did *not* mitigate his sheer stupidity. What the hell had he been thinking? Taking Brooke to the apartment before the area had been cleared by the FBI forensic experts almost got her killed. Evidence had been destroyed. Any hope of keeping the investigation quiet had vanished in a puff of ugly black smoke. He'd half expected to see news trucks encamped outside Brooke's house, but there was nothing yet. For now, the media was focused on the bomb and the fire, but it was only a matter of time before they made the connection with Layla and the so-called Hardy Dolls. As the assistant director had reminded him and Keller, this was a high-profile case.

After identifying himself to the cop parked at the curb, Sloan marched up the sidewalk to the front door. All things considered, his meetings at headquarters had gone well. SAC Keller had cut him some slack, allowing him to stay on the case—strictly in a profiling capacity—instead of recommending disciplinary action. To be realistic, Keller's decision wasn't all luck. He was also protecting his own ass. Sloan had advised him that he intended to go to Layla's apartment, and Keller hadn't raised an objection.

Neither of them had expected a goddamned bomb.

The explosive device didn't fit the profile for a killer who had transported Layla to the cabin and carefully, almost lovingly, arranged her body. Brooke's observations about a nearly unnotice-able search stood in direct contrast to the explo-sion. A bomb was the opposite of subtle. If the killer meant to blow everything up, why was he so careful not to trash the apartment?

As soon as Sloan pressed the doorbell, Gimbel answered. Though still grinning, the old man looked ragged around the edges. "Get in here," he growled. "It's after my ten o'clock bedtime, and somebody who is more awake needs to handle these women."

"Franny and Brooke?"

"And the twins, Moira and Megan. And Megan's four-year-old daughter, Emily, who finally went to sleep." He hooked his thumbs in his red suspenders and rocked back on his heels. "If their chatter isn't enough to drive you straight up the wall, Tom Lancaster just got here."

"From what I recall, you recommended him."

"Tom's a decent guy, not contentious. He's not a trial lawyer—more of a paper pusher who does estate planning and property law."

"Why is he here?"

"Brooke called him. She wants to hire a security firm, which means she needs to access funds from their joint account."

Sloan had a few questions about how that account worked. Brooke seemed to think that their funds were unlimited. "Earlier today, Brooke mentioned that Lancaster called her. Did he say anything about business he had with Layla?"

"I haven't interviewed him," Gimbel said. "That's your job. But I can give you a heads-up. The lawyer might have been the last person to speak to Layla a couple of days ago. One of the twins had a message from Layla and tried to call back, but they didn't connect."

Sloan had spoken on the phone to both twins but hadn't met them in person. He heard voices from the kitchen. Somebody sounded angry, but he couldn't identify the voice. "What can you tell me about Megan and Moira?"

"You first," Gimbel said. "I want to hear about the bomb."

"We won't know details until the ATFE experts are done investigating, but the preliminary report says that the device was triggered when we opened the door. A fairly sophisticated mechanism but not brilliant, it was set to detonate fifteen minutes after somebody turned the key in the lock."

"A booby trap," Gimbel said. "You can't blame yourself for what happened. Anybody could have set off the bomb."

"But it wasn't just anybody. It was me."

And he should have known better. Sloan had come to Denver with a reputation for being an effective agent with training as a profiler, but he'd pulled an epic fail on his first investigation. He'd missed the signs that this guy was a bomber. According to the four women in the other room, he was also a prank caller and possibly a stalker.

The conversation in the kitchen got louder as the women argued. When Sloan glanced longingly toward the exit, Gimbel chuckled. "I feel like a grandpa," he said. "These ladies are interesting but a little crazy. I'm glad they're not my problem."

"They're my problem?"

"You're their designated handler." He gestured down the hall toward the kitchen. "Nothing to worry about—it's just four deeply traumatized women who are scared out of their minds and in mourning for their dead friend."

"Piece of cake," he muttered.

In the kitchen, Franny and a woman with a long black braid sat on high stools on one side of the polished marble-topped island. Lancaster left an open stool between himself and Franny. Brooke stood opposite them, nearest the sink. The fourth woman paced at the far end of the island, speaking nonstop about how she refused, absolutely refused to have a bodyguard interfere in her busy life.

Noticing him, she stopped midsentence. All four women stared with their identical blue eyes. Though their features were unique, except for the twins, they resembled each other enough that he was both fascinated and unsettled. Twelve years ago, when Martin Hardy assembled his family of dolls, he'd chosen carefully to make a matched set. They all had black hair, but the styles were different.

Brooke introduced him and welcomed him into their circle. Tom Lancaster—a skinny, nervous-looking guy with a shaven head and heavy glasses—rose from his stool and shook hands. None of the women made a similar offer. He understood why they might distrust him. He'd failed to save Layla and had put Brooke in danger.

"I want to speak with each of you separately," he said. "Your experiences and observations are integral to developing a profile of the killer."

"There's only one thing I need to know." Megan ceased her pacing, braced her palms on the marble countertop and glared at him. "Is there a danger to me and my daughter?"

"Duh!" Her twin, Moira, flipped her long braid. "Layla's dead, murdered. And a bomb nearly killed Brooke. If that isn't danger, what is?"

"You're no expert." Megan's smooth, precision-cut bob and bangs shone in the glow from the overhead track lighting. "Special Agent Sloan has been trained to deal with violent danger and death, right?"

He'd never heard his job described that way. "If you're wondering about the need for full-time protection, I believe you'd be well advised to hire a bodyguard."

"Thank you," Brooke said emphatically. "I've arranged for us to meet with two different security firms tonight."

She went on to describe how the bodyguard duties would be arranged with one guard at her house, where she and Franny would be staying, another for Moira, and another for Megan and her daughter. Megan was quick to point out that if her husband were in town instead of on a tour of duty in the Middle East, he could protect them.

"Yeah, yeah, yeah," Moira droned. "We all know that your Special Forces stud could dominate any psycho killer. Lucky you, Megan."

"I don't tempt fate," she snapped at her twin. "Not like you. I don't go floating around to Wiccan events or dance naked in the full moon."

"You have your kind of protection and I have mine."

Throughout the sisterly exchange, Franny was uncharacteristically quiet, with her eyes averted, looking down. Sloan appreciated when Gimbel circled the island and stood beside the curly-haired pixie who wore a crown of silk flowers—red roses and rosemary for remembrance. She slid from her stool, wrapped her arms around Gimbel and buried her face against his barrel chest.

With her ADD and bipolar tendencies, Franny tended to be demonstrative, vividly expressing her emotions. At any given moment, she might burst into tears or launch a medley of show tunes. The tricky part to understanding her would be reading the subtext.

Sloan didn't know what to expect from the twins. According to Gimbel, they both suffered from depression. Megan—with her husband and daughter—appeared to be a typical soccer mom but she had an edge and it didn't take much to ignite her rage. The main thing she had in common with her twin was involvement in charity work. Megan volunteered at various veterans' groups and homeless shelters, while Moira focused on the arts, raising money for a dance troupe and being a docent at the art museum. She also did some oil painting and was known for disappearing from sight for weeks at a time.

"Agent Sloan," Megan snapped, "you don't need a private interview with me. We can talk right now. Let's get it over with."

"I don't work that way." After his negligence at Layla's apartment, he meant to play his role as an investigator by the book. Turning to Brooke, he asked, "Can I use your office?"

"Wasting time," Megan said. "I'll tell you what happened. The last time I had contact with Layla was two and a half weeks ago. She came to my daughter's soccer game and brought oranges for treats. It would have been nice if she'd cut the fruit into smaller pieces, but she knew nothing about raising children."

"How would she? Layla didn't have kids." Moira scowled. "And she didn't have much of a childhood. None of us did."

"Layla was sixteen when Hardy took her. We were eleven."

Franny pulled away from Gimbel. "You two

were the last taken. You don't know what it was like before you got there."

"Stop bickering," Brooke said. "This is why Sloan wanted to talk to us alone. If we're in a group, we interrupt each other."

He took his spiral notebook from his inner jacket pocket. "Come with me, Brooke. We'll go to your office."

With a brisk nod, she came out from behind the island. "If any of you want more to drink or eat, help yourselves. Franny knows where everything is kept."

Brushing past him, she went down the hall to the office, where, he noticed, she'd been smart enough to lower the blinds, hiding the interior of her house from outside threats. She'd changed into a white button-down shirt and khaki shorts—a plain, practical outfit that she somehow made sexy. Her long black hair hung loosely to her shoulders, and she was barefoot. For some reason, she was still wearing her fanny pack.

"Have you left the house?" he asked.

"Not since the officer brought me home from Layla's apartment." She closed the door and leaned against it, not retreating behind her desk. "I've had my hands full with Franny and the others. Why do you ask?"

"You're wearing your fanny pack."

Her eyebrows lifted, and her lips spread in a cool, clever smile. "There's a reason."

He should have been asking questions, digging for the truth, but she disarmed his professional intentions. In spite of his bad judgment at Layla's apartment and his inability to get a grip on a profile for the killer, he experienced a profound sense of happiness when he looked at her and heard her voice. "I'm glad you're okay."

"Back at you." She unzipped the fanny pack, reached inside and pulled out a small padded container. "Surprise!"

She'd grabbed the case of thumb drives from inside Layla's desk. Because of her quick thinking, that evidence survived the blast. "Brooke, you're a genius."

"I know."

Chapter Eight

Brooke kept her smile small and restrained. In the midst of tragedy, an excessive display of joy would be gross and inappropriate. But she couldn't help beaming inside. She liked when he'd called her a genius. Having Sloan acknowledge her intelligence was an even better compliment than if he'd raved about her body or her hair or the blue of her eyes. Her eye color seemed especially unimportant—nothing more than a genetic trait she'd inherited from parents who hadn't cared enough about her to stick around.

"I should tell you," she said, "that I grabbed the case with the thumb drives before you found the bomb. My plan was to take it whether or not you approved. It's a keepsake. The data will remind me of Layla."

"And it's evidence," he said.

"That, too."

"Is it possible that you swiped evidence because you don't trust the FBI to do a good job of investigating?"

More than possible! The way she figured, Layla's murderer was someone who slipped through the net on the first FBI investigation. She blamed the institution and the bureaucracy. But not him. "All due respect, Sloan, I'm sure you're competent."

He looked down at the padded case in his hand with the sort of reverence that was usually given to a precious artifact. His gaze lifted, and he connected with her. "I'm not proud of the way I've handled the investigation. Never should have taken you to Layla's apartment. Never should have gone inside until the forensic experts gave the all clear. If you'd been injured in the blast, it would have been my fault."

"But I wasn't. Not hurt. I'm perfectly fine." After her years of therapy, Brooke recognized his guilt-ridden mea culpa as a sign of an overprotective nature. She shared those control issues. "Besides, if we hadn't gone to the apartment, we would have had to wait a long time for the forensic people to tell us about Channing, the little twerp."

"Give the CSIs some credit," he said. "They would have discovered Peter's emails pretty quickly."

"Would they have shared that information with you? Would you have told me?"

"Yes and yes. I'm not taking part in the active

investigation, but it's understood that I need access to all the evidence to create a profile."

"Speaking of which, when can we see Peter Channing?"

He didn't flinch at her demand, but he didn't applaud, either. "I'll have to check with SAC Keller. He's running the show."

Not good enough. She was impatient to move forward. The longer the investigation dragged on, the longer she and her friends were in danger. Channing was the most obvious suspect. His childhood connection to all of them was creepy to say the least, and he'd been reaching out to Layla, trying to establish a line of communication.

"I need to talk to him face-to-face."

If he'd murdered her friend, she wanted revenge. Nothing would make her happier than to see Channing locked in the prison cell next door to his uncle. A sick, disgusting family reunion was exactly what they deserved.

Martin Hardy's trial had taken place when she was only fifteen, and she'd never had the chance to appear in open court. Testifying in judge's chambers wasn't as satisfying as taking the witness stand and pointing at the monster who had ruined her life. *J'accuse, you bastard.*

"When we have him in custody, I'll do what I can to set up an interview," Sloan said. "But we need to follow the rules."

"I agree."

"That means I have to turn these thumb drives over to Keller."

"Wait!" She went toward him. Her hand rested on the sleeve of his blazer as if she could stop him with a touch. "Shouldn't I have a say in what happens? I had the foresight to take the thumb drives. At the very least, I should have a chance to look at the contents."

"You're a witness, not a detective."

"But I can help."

"Rules," he said.

"What could it hurt for me to take a look?"

His jaw tensed. She figured that he'd refuse to share the evidence. The cops and the feds—even Gimbel—were oh-so-secretive about their investigation. She shouldn't expect Sloan to be different from the others.

He surprised her by handing the case back to her. "As long as I'm not putting you in danger, there's no harm done. I won't tell Keller about the thumb drives until after I interview Franny, Megan and Moira. That gives you enough time to make copies."

Standing close to him, she glanced up and whispered a thank-you. After all they'd been through today, he should have been frazzled, but he still appeared calm and collected. The only sign of disarray was a shadow of stubble on his jaw. "Do you always wear a suit?"

"Not always. When I get shot with pepper spray, I strip down."

If that was all it took to get him undressed, she could snatch the pepper spray out of her fanny pack right now. "There must be a less painful way to make you relax."

"We could experiment."

The husky note in his voice alerted her to what was really happening between them. They were flirting. Not an unusual occurrence for a typical twenty-six-year-old woman. But she never made suggestive remarks or batted her eyelashes or flashed her cleavage. Flirting with a fed? Unheard of! And yet, with her free hand, she reached for his striped necktie and gave a tug.

"Maybe you could loosen this knot," she said.

Without breaking eye contact, he reached up and wrenched the knot lower. He unfastened the first button on his light blue shirt. "This feels better."

Her lips parted, and her pulse accelerated. She found it hard to swallow. Her reaction wasn't due to a panic attack. She was aroused, sensually aroused. Her tummy churned. A heated flush crept up her throat, and she knew she must be blushing.

Brooke had experienced fully consummated sex with penetration exactly three times in her life. The first time was out of curiosity—a desire to find out what all the hype was about. She'd researched, selected a suitable partner and propositioned him. The results disappointed her. She was *not* overwhelmed by ecstasy, the earth did *not* move and she didn't hear a symphonic crescendo. The second time—with the same guy—had been undertaken in an attempt to improve. It wasn't a zero but certainly not a ten. After her third try with a different mate, she decided that she just wasn't someone who enjoyed sex.

Standing close to Sloan and watching him loosen his necktie caused a more thrilling response, a trembling from deep inside. Maybe the danger had cranked her endorphins into high gear. Maybe his protective nature turned her on. Or maybe the timing was right. Whatever the reason, she wanted him.

With a gentle caress, he brushed a wisp of hair off her cheek and tucked it behind her ear. The silver facets in his gray eyes sparkled and shimmered. Whether this was sexual magic or some kind of delusion, she liked it and leaned even closer to him, close enough that she could smell the smoke from the explosion that still clung to his clothes. The danger was real. She shouldn't allow herself to be distracted. But their bodies were almost touching.

There was a tap on the door. She heard Lancaster call her name. "What is it?"

"A representative from the security firm is here."

Though irritated by the interruption, she was

also a little bit relieved. To Sloan, she said, "I have to deal with this. The rep from this company agreed to come over tonight, even though it's after ten."

"Bodyguards are used to working odd hours."

Her eyelids squeezed shut, and her lips pinched. The moment with Sloan had passed. Now it was time for her to get back to the business of managing everybody else. She responded to Lancaster, "I'll be right there."

The attorney pushed open the door and poked his head inside. "If you want, I can handle the hiring. That's why you wanted me to come over, isn't it?"

"Not really." Though she viewed him through the sensual haze of her attraction to Sloan, Tom Lancaster had less appeal than a long-tailed gecko. His shaved head sloped down to thick glasses that magnified his eyes. He was skinny and fidgety. How dare he suppose that she couldn't take care of hiring the security firm? "I know what I want."

"I'm just saying." He shrugged his narrow shoulders. "I've worked with this company before. They're the ones I recommended to install your security cameras and locks."

She'd been satisfied with their work but had gone with a more experienced team to design and build her panic room in the basement. "I'll talk to the rep."

"Just trying to help," he said. "Tell me what to do, and I'm on it."

"Come over early tomorrow. I need your help to put Layla's affairs in order. For now, you might as well go home."

Sloan stepped forward. "Before you go, I have a few questions for you."

She shooed both men toward the door. "If you don't mind, I'd like to use my office for the interview with the security rep. Agent Sloan, I'd advise you to talk to Franny first. When we were growing up, she had the most contact with Peter."

Before he exited, Sloan gave her a wink so quick and unexpected that she almost missed it. If he was flirting again, she had to admit—grudgingly—that she approved.

As Sloan accompanied the lawyer to the front foyer, he took the spiral notebook from his pocket to record Lancaster's answers. He didn't expect this to be a deep discussion, but Lancaster might have been the last person to have contact with Layla. Sloan wanted that information to construct a timeline. "You had an appointment with Layla. When was the last time you talked to her?"

Lancaster pushed his glasses up on his nose and shot an angry glance over his shoulder toward the kitchen, where they could hear the women introducing themselves to the rep from the security firm. "This is typical of Brooke. She refuses to ask anybody else for help, thinks she can do it all herself. She should have let me handle the business with the rep."

"There are specific issues she wants covered." Without thinking twice, Sloan defended Brooke. "She can take care of the hiring."

"Can she?"

The glow from the chandelier in the entryway reflected off his shaved dome, making his head seem too big for the rest of his body. Sloan smiled to himself, wondering if the oversize noggin was a literal manifestation of an ego-driven personality. "Brooke seems like a competent businesswoman."

"Oh, sure, she likes to think she's in control, but I can tell she's upset. Didn't you see how her fingers were trembling? She was breathing hard and blushing—all signs that she's scared to death."

Sloan had a fair idea of what was going on inside Brooke, and it wasn't fear. After their intimate moment in her office, his heart thumped in double time. He was turned on, and he guessed that she felt much the same. "There are many possible reasons she could be agitated."

"You barely know her. I've spent time with these girls, watched them grow into women, and I don't mind telling you that I'm worried. Layla's murder is going to have an effect." He jabbed a long, skinny finger at the center of Sloan's chest.

"You need to catch the killer, and you need to do it fast."

As if he had intended to drag his feet? Sloan had already gotten himself into trouble once by rushing into Layla's apartment instead of waiting for the forensic people. Speed wasn't as important as doing the investigation right. A lawyer ought to understand, but not this guy. Sloan was beginning to take a serious dislike to Lancaster. "Rest assured that the FBI will handle the investigation with all due haste."

"I should hope so."

"Again, I'm asking you. When was the last time you had contact with Layla?"

"I spoke to her on the phone three days ago, on Tuesday. Hang on and I'll tell you exactly what time."

Lancaster opened an app on his phone and scrolled down the screen. Waiting in silence, Sloan could hear the conversation from the kitchen but didn't recognize the tone of Brooke's voice. She'd probably taken the rep into her office.

He stared at the lawyer, who continued to play with his phone. Keeping Sloan waiting was a power play, a way to show that his time was more important. "Never mind, I'll contact your office."

"Here it is. My phone consultation with Layla lasted from 1:16 to 1:33 on Tuesday, and it fell into the category of billable hours."

His statement fit with what Brooke had told him. "What did you talk about?"

"Not so fast, Agent Sloan. Let's not forget attorney-client privilege."

The pretentious lawyer enjoyed thwarting the FBI investigation while simultaneously demanding immediate answers. Sloan's dislike for Lancaster was rapidly turning into hostility. "If you don't cooperate, I'll take you into custody for questioning."

"You wouldn't dare."

Sloan drew himself up to his full height, a good five inches taller than bigheaded Lancaster. "According to Brooke, Layla was looking for an office to lease. My assumption was that she contacted you, her lawyer and the administrator of the group funds, to make sure she had the financial wherewithal."

"I'm not saying." Lancaster gave a smug little smirk.

"It's been one hell of a day. I'm in no mood to dance."

"Too bad."

As a general rule, Sloan tried to avoid exerting his authority, but Lancaster and his phony attitude made him want to hammer the lawyer, watch him crumple to the ground and drag his limp remains to jail. "Last chance to cooperate."

"I've got to respect the rule of law."

"Turn around, put your hands behind your back."

He yelped, "What?"

"Your reluctance to discuss such a banal matter makes me think you have something to hide." Sloan wasn't carrying handcuffs, but he had a couple of zip ties in the pocket of his blazer. He took them out and dangled them from his forefinger. "Your refusal to answer my questions amounts to obstruction of justice on a time-sensitive case where the safety of other people is threatened."

"It's my right."

"And I'm within my jurisdiction to arrest you."

Sloan heard a gasp. He turned and saw Franny, Moira and Megan standing in the doorway, watching the argument. Their blue eyes were wide, curious. He gave the ladies a nod. "Sorry you had to see this."

"Tell him." Lancaster stamped his foot on the tiled floor. "You ladies need to tell him how much I've helped you and taken care of you. I'm like a father."

Franny shook her head. "Not that I have experience with fathers, but I don't think so."

Lancaster continued, "I managed your funds brilliantly. Whenever you needed money, it was there for school fees and down payments. Never once have I turned you down."

"That's not true," Moira said. "You refused to make a ten-thousand-dollar donation to my friends who needed to rent space for a dance concert."

"I borrowed from our joint account for the down payment on my house," Megan said, "but I paid the money back."

Sloan found it interesting that the women weren't defending the attorney who had handled their affairs for twelve years. Lancaster wasn't winning any popularity contests with this group. Had Layla argued with him?

He intended to take a closer look at Lancaster, possibly to subpoena the records for the fund he managed. He clamped his hand around the lawyer's scrawny arm. "You need to come with me."

"You don't have to do this. I'll cooperate." Behind his glasses, his eyes flickered from the left to the right. "When Layla called, she wanted to know if funds were available to lease an office. She gave me a ballpark figure, and I gave her my approval."

"Why did she need your approval?" Moira demanded. "It's our money."

Anger tinged her voice. When he'd turned her down for the dance company donation, he'd made an enemy. Sloan focused on Lancaster. "According to what you told me, the phone call was over fifteen minutes long. What else did you talk about?"

"She wanted my advice as a lawyer on whether she should join a group or go into private practice. I gave her my opinion and a few referrals to other young lawyers. Anything else I can tell you?"

"I advise you not to leave town until this investigation is over."

"Fine."

As soon as Sloan released him, the lawyer stomped to the front door and waited for Franny to enter the code to deactivate the alarm. Lancaster left without saying goodbye to his clients. Before she could scamper back to the others, Sloan spoke to her. "I have a few questions for you."

"Nothing to say." She covered her mouth with both fists.

"Please, Franny. We can go someplace quiet."

"Fine, we'll go to the basement." She gestured, and he followed. Halfway down the staircase, she turned and said, "You need to catch him."

"Who?"

"Peter Channing."

Chapter Nine

If Sloan had been more alert, he would have re-membered that the shooting range was in the basement. Before he could suggest a quieter place, Franny had skipped down the hallway and used a code to unlock the door to the soundproofed range. Inside the well-lit but sparsely furnished room, there was another code to access a locked case holding an array of handguns.

He wanted to question Franny about her direct accusation of Channing, but she had dropped that topic and moved on. Humming to herself, she reached into the case and selected a Walther P22 with a pink handle and frame.

"This will help me relax," she said with a cheery grin. "Shooting gives me focus. When I take aim, I have to clear my brain and concen-trate. Moira says it's like meditation."

He'd never heard of Zen target practice before, but it made sense for someone like Franny, whose bipolar tendencies could send her mind scampering in many directions. While she aimed and fired at a target, her field of interest was limited.

"I understand," he said. "Before we start talking, I want to tell you that I'm sorry about what happened to Layla. It's hard to lose such a close friend."

"I haven't cried yet. The tears are right there, but they won't come out." Her smile wavered. "Brooke told us she was already dead before I tried to reach her on the phone."

"I haven't developed a timeline yet, but you can be sure that there was nothing you could have done to stop the murder."

"Maybe or maybe not." She pivoted and went to a counter where two shooting areas were separated by a partition. As she loaded a clip into her automatic, she said, "If you want, you can fire your own weapon. I bet you're pretty good."

This was a competition he didn't want to start. "I'd rather watch."

She squinted down the lane at a paper target of a human silhouette with a bull's-eye superimposed on the torso. The distance from the counter looked to be twenty-five or thirty yards. Sloan had no doubt that Brooke had been responsible for this setup, from selection of a target that mimicked the human form to the distance. Fifty yards would be a more challenging shot, and if Franny was training to be a sniper, the greater distance would be important. Mastering twenty-five yards was better for self-defense.

Franny removed her crown of roses and rosemary to put on noise-canceling headphones. She pointed to a second pair. "Those are for you. It gets loud in here."

In her paisley blouse, cutoff jean shorts and red cowboy boots, she looked perky and carefree, but her stance when she aimed her weapon was all business. In less than two minutes, she'd emptied the magazine and reloaded. After another ten shots, she turned away from the target.

Her cheeks were flushed, and she was gasping for air. Many gun novices held their breath while they fired. Her eyes were bright as she pulled off the headphones.

"Peter Channing," she said. "Three months ago, I thought I saw him in a grocery store."

"You were kids when you knew him." Sloan adapted to her change in topic. "He was only eleven years old. He must have changed."

"This guy wore his hair short, just like Peter when he was a kid. And he had the same lopsided grin with a dimple on one side." The words gushed from her. "He was skinny—Peter was always skinny. When we were kids, I could wrap my arms all the way around him. He didn't see me in the grocery store."

"Did you approach him?"

"The opposite. I wanted to run away and hide,

but then I wondered if I had the right guy. It's happened to me before. I'll catch a glimpse from the corner of my eye, and I'll be sure—I mean, totally sure—that it's Hardy coming after me with his big, jagged hunting knife. Even though I know he's locked up in jail, I think he's there until I get closer and see that I'm wrong. So I decided to follow the guy in the grocery store."

"If you ever feel threatened again, you can call me or emergency services."

"You sound like Brooke. She has nine-one-one on speed dial."

As he well remembered, Brooke hadn't hesitated to hit that call button and lash out with her canister of pepper spray. He was curious about how she'd convinced unicorn-loving Franny to pick up a handgun and shoot. Later he might ask. Right now, he refused to be sidetracked. The focus was on Peter Channing. "Tell me about how you trailed him."

"I ducked behind the cantaloupe," she said, "went past the dairy and the meat. In the frozen food aisle, he picked out three pizzas. That made me think he was a bachelor."

"Good reasoning."

"It was springtime, and he was wearing baggy shorts. I tried to get close enough to see if he had a scar on his calf. That would have been positive identification. One time when we were playing, he got tangled in the long chain that tethered my ankle to the bedframe. Peter fell against the fire-place. He had a terrible gash. It was bleeding and bleeding and I couldn't make it stop. If Mr. Hardy came in and saw what happened to his nephew, I'd be punished. He'd already cut off the top of my finger, and I didn't know what would come next. Peter saved me."

"How?"

"He ran out the door into the forest and pre-tended that he got hurt out there. His uncle be-lieved him, and I didn't get blamed." Her forehead twisted into a frown. "Peter was my hero, but he was also my captor. At any given time, he could have talked to the police and rescued me and the others."

Her story reminded him of Stockholm syn-drome, when hostages became deeply attached to their kidnappers. Her insight added a layer of complexity to an emerging profile of Peter Chan-ning. "Did he want to be your hero?"

"Oh, yeah. We played lots of games where I was a princess and he had to fight a dragon to save me."

"Was he in love with you?"

"We were ten and eleven years old. Too young to be in love." A tremor in her voice hinted at an emotional connection, and he wondered how many times she'd been in love. The intense child-hood trauma had to affect her relationships with men. "We were just friends."

Sloan shifted the topic. "Did you see the scar on his leg?"

"I never got close enough. When he went into the parking lot, I lost track of him." She quickly reloaded her pink pistol and fired one shot without the headphones. "I don't know if I really saw him, but I couldn't stay in my apartment near the grocery store. I moved before the end of the month."

"Why didn't you call the FBI?"

"I wasn't sure, and I didn't want to be the girl who cried wolf."

"When you started getting the crank phone calls, did you recognize the voice?"

"I don't know if it was Peter." Though she wasn't crying, she dabbed at the corner of her eye. "His voice would have changed a lot, so I can't tell. The person who called repeated things Mr. Hardy said to me about how little ladies had to behave or else they'd be punished. I could lose another finger or a toe or an arm."

Her self-control was slipping. He needed to rein her in. "Before we came down to the basement, you said I needed to catch Channing. Why were you so sure?"

"The killer is from our past." Her conviction was strong, and she sounded angry. "You need to arrest Peter. Who else could it be?"

He remembered Brooke's story about the

face at the window. "Do you remember Zachary Doyle?"

"The creepy neighbor," she said. "I didn't know his name until the trial, and I only saw him peeping in the window once. He was more interested in Brooke and Layla and Sophia."

Though Sloan didn't have a psychological workup on Doyle or any of the other men who had visited Hardy's cabin, they seemed to be a better fit for the profile of a killer who had terrorized the other girls and killed Layla. Their sexual experience, twelve years ago, would have made an indelible impression.

The little boy who'd played with Franny didn't seem to have a clear motivation, but the fact that Layla hadn't been sexually molested pointed to Channing. He might think his relationships with the women were pure. He considered himself to be their hero. If he had engaged in crank calls and weird stalking, he meant to frighten them so that he could, when the time was right, come to their rescue.

A buzzer sounded, indicating that someone was at the door to the shooting gallery. When he opened the door, Moira immediately grasped his hand and pulled him along with her. "You've got to come quickly. Brooke is going to kill him."

He knew better than to ask what was going on. If Brooke believed that the only way to protect her friends was murder, he had no doubt that she was capable.

SITTING BEHIND HER DESK, Brooke aimed her Glock at the bearded middle-aged man who looked like he was trying to be a young hipster in his skinny jeans, combat boots and fedora. Nick Brancusi, documentary filmmaker, had bluffed his way into her house by pretending to be a rep from one of the security firms she had contacted.

At first, the manicured beard and mustache had thrown her off, and he'd talked a good game in describing bodyguard services. But his presentation had sounded too slick, and she'd smelled a phony. As soon as she recognized him, Brooke invited him into her office, told him to sit, took out her gun and aimed. Icky Nicky probably wasn't feeling so glib right now.

"Let me explain," he said.

"No talking." She sighted down the barrel of her gun. This should have been a nerve-racking confrontation, but she was experiencing a profound sense of inner peace. She hated the threat and the danger it posed, but she loved being in control.

"Come on, Brooke, just listen to me."

She bounded to her feet and stood behind the desk. Glaring down at him, she struck a two-handed shooter's pose. Her fingers didn't tremble. The adrenaline pumping through her veins elevated her pulse, but she was breathing easily. *No panic attack here!* "I don't want to hear anything you have to say. Don't beg."

"This is a legit business opportunity."

"Save it, Nicky. There's an FBI agent in the basement. He'll be here any minute, and he will take you into custody."

"Protective custody," Brancusi muttered. "I hope he can keep me safe from you."

It would serve him right if she shot the fedora off his head, but that would ruin the wall and she didn't want to spackle. "Not another word."

When Sloan entered the office with Moira and Franny following close behind, he quickly assessed what was going on, and he grinned. "I appreciate your alert action, Brooke. I'll take it from here."

She slipped her Glock into the desk drawer and locked it. "The creep is all yours, Special Agent Sloan."

His expression darkened as he confronted Nick Brancusi. "Show me your ID."

"I never meant any harm." He slouched lower in the chair as though trying to make himself disappear. "I'm a documentarian."

When Brancusi reached into his vest pocket, Sloan drew his weapon. Towering and threatening, the nose of his gun was less than a foot from Brancusi's forehead. "What do you think you're doing?"

"Reaching for my passport." He held up both hands. "It's in my pocket."

"On your feet," Sloan growled. "Now."

Brancusi stood, but his nerves wouldn't let him keep still. He shifted back and forth from one foot to the other in a cowardly dance that pleased Brooke no end. She truly disliked this man who had exploited their childhood trauma.

"I haven't done anything wrong," Brancusi protested. "I'm here with a business deal."

"Were you invited?"

"Not exactly."

"How did you get into the house?" Sloan demanded.

"I pretended to be from a security firm."

"You entered under false pretenses."

"Well, yes." Brancusi's hands were still raised. "I wanted a chance to make my pitch. I have a pretty good offer for a follow-up documentary on the Hardy Dolls, especially since Layla is, you know…"

Franny squeezed her eyelids shut and threw her head back. A high-pitched keening noise squeezed past her clenched teeth. A violent tremor shook her shoulders and went all the way down to her feet. *Poor Franny!* This was tearing her apart. She felt everything so deeply.

Brooke rushed around the desk and gathered her friend in her arms. Together, she and Moira guided her to the sofa by the window, where she collapsed in a boneless heap.

Her wailing continued. "She's dead. Layla's dead."

Her outburst was disturbing, but Brooke understood what was happening, and she actually approved. Holding too much grief inside was difficult and painful, especially for a gentle soul like Franny, who desperately needed to vent.

Embracing her friend, Brooke patted Franny on the back while her cries subsided and she wept. This was a difficult balancing act. Brooke needed to take care of Franny. At the same time, she had to follow the investigation and help Sloan. Finding Layla's murderer took precedence over everything else…if there truly was anything she could do.

She watched Sloan intently.

"You make me sick," he said to the filmmaker. "You planned to use Layla's death for publicity."

"Hey, it's not my choice. I'm just giving people what they want. The media is going to be looking for answers, and I happen to be an expert on what happened to these ladies."

"I'm taking you in for questioning."

"I don't see why."

"You've got a motive. You might have killed Layla for the great publicity."

"You've got to believe me when I say I haven't done anything wrong." His cynicism vanished.

His voice sounded meek and complaisant, but she remembered that he had been an actor before becoming a filmmaker. Nothing he said could be trusted. "Am I under arrest?"

"Not yet."

"I'll come quietly. You don't need cuffs."

"Technically, I don't," Sloan said, "but I want to use them."

It was obvious that Sloan wasn't buying Brancusi's phony innocent act. He continued, "I want you restrained so you can know what it's like to be caught, trapped with no hope of escape. If the FBI wants you in jail overnight, that's where you'll be. And your confinement is nothing compared to the trauma suffered by these women. Their abuse wasn't a movie, a game or a stunt. And I won't let you treat them like victims. They're survivors, and I never want to hear you call them 'dolls' again."

Brooke mentally applauded every word he said. Sloan came close to understanding the damage that had been done to them. The ordeal started with Martin Hardy and continued after they had escaped. Every time they were recognized or their names came up in the media, they were thrown into the inescapable past and weren't allowed to forget. Sloan's empathy came from a deeper source than psychological training. She wondered if he had undergone a similar trauma.

Leaving Franny with Moira, she crossed the

room toward Sloan as he tightened the zip ties on Brancusi's wrists and escorted him out of the office. Standing in the front entryway under the chandelier, Sloan made a phone call. There was no need for him to hold on to Brancusi's arm. Those tiny zip ties were enough to restrain the documentarian, who stood silently with his head drooping forward and his gaze focused on his combat boots.

When Sloan finished his call, she asked, "Where are you taking him?"

"Headquarters," he said. "Will you input the code to turn off the door alarms?"

"I should be with you for the questioning." In her heart, she didn't really believe that Icky Nicky was capable of murder, but he might know something vital. "I don't want to be cut out of the investigation."

"I'll stay in touch," he said.

Brooke knew when she was being blown off. Sloan was trying to dump her. She didn't intend to sit quietly and let that happen. "I'll meet you at headquarters."

"It's late, after midnight. Might be best if you stay here and take care of Franny."

He made a good point. Brooke had always tended the pains and sorrows of her friends. As foster kids, they'd all been abandoned by their families, which gave her strong motivation to be steadfast and loyal. She couldn't leave Franny when she was so upset. With a frustrated sigh, she tapped the keypad to disengage the alarm and held the door for Sloan to make his exit.

Standing on the front stoop, she watched as he approached the police car parked at the curb and handed Brancusi over to the cop on duty. The soles of her feet itched to race down the sidewalk and jump into the passenger side of his SUV before he pulled away. She and her friends had been threatened, and she needed to know everything—every tiny detail—about what had happened.

Franny stepped onto the stoop beside her. Her eyes were red and puffy, but the tears had stopped. She held Brooke's fanny pack. "Your keys are inside. Go."

"Are you okay?"

"I'll manage."

"But I need to talk to the security firms."

"Tomorrow is soon enough."

That was true. With a couple of phone calls, Brooke could postpone the meetings. "Are you sure you're all right?"

"There's nothing you can do to change my grief. Go," Franny said. "Find the monster who killed Layla."

That was precisely what she intended to do.

Chapter Ten

After a conversation with SAC Keller at FBI headquarters, Sloan returned to the fourth-floor conference room where he'd left Brooke. At one end of the room was a conversation area with a long rectangular brown sofa, chairs and a coffee table. The other end was set up for demonstrations with whiteboards, easels and a pull-down screen for PowerPoint presentations. The long table in the middle was used for briefings and meetings. Through the windows that lined the west wall, he could see the distant lights of downtown Denver.

During his absence, she'd made herself comfortable, curling up on the sofa and kicking off her shoes. Her head rested on the arm of the sofa, which she'd cushioned with her ubiquitous fanny pack. Her eyes were closed. He lowered himself into the chair beside the sofa and exhaled a heavy breath. Today had been intense, and the pressure didn't show any sign of easing. He was exhausted, running on fumes.

Special Agent in Charge Keller and his boss, Martinez, weren't real happy with Sloan's decision to share information with Brooke and use her as a resource. He had to admit that their doubts were reasonable, because he couldn't be certain that he was doing the right thing for her. Even though she insisted on taking part, an investigation could be traumatic and dangerous—as evidenced by the bomb in Layla's apartment.

He watched her as she slept. Her white shirt had come untucked, and he caught a glimpse of her smooth skin above her waist. Her expression was untroubled, peaceful. Black lashes formed crescents on her cheeks. Her full, pink lips parted slightly.

Rousing her from a sound sleep could be a problem. Some people who had been hostages reacted badly if jolted awake. Their barely conscious minds flashed back to the trauma, and they lashed out. He had no desire to be on the receiving end of another Brooke attack. And so he sat quietly, waiting and watching until her eyelids fluttered and opened.

Immediately alert, she bolted upright. "How long have you been sitting there?"

"A couple of minutes."

"Watching me while I sleep? Kind of creepy, Sloan."

Or prudent. It was entirely possible that she'd

wake with a start and blast him with pepper spray. "Can I get you something to drink?"

She shook her head. "When do we start questioning Brancusi?"

"As soon as we figure out a timeline we can use to check his alibi."

"Let's get to it." She jumped off the sofa, slipped her feet into her espadrilles and charged toward the opposite end of the room with the whiteboards. She picked up a marker and wrote the word *Monday* on the board. "We'll start here. Layla called me in the morning. She was planning to rent office space and wanted me to come with her to an appointment on Friday."

He sauntered toward the whiteboard, impressed by her vigorous show of energy. "Organization comes naturally to you."

"Too much?"

"It's a good quality," he said. "I like that you set up our timeline on a whiteboard. And I'm in awe of the way you've got everything you need in that fanny pack."

"Good." She grinned as she smoothed a wisp of her hair back into her ponytail. "I've always been like this and don't think I can change. *Organized* sounds much nicer than *displaying OCD tendencies*."

"You're not crazy," he said. "Maybe a little bit annoying, but not psychotic."

"Professional opinion?"

Actually, it was. He had the necessary qualifications and training to be a therapist. "In your Monday phone call with Layla, what else did you talk about?"

"She had concerns about starting a solo career but didn't want to join a group of other lawyers until she knew them better. And she meant to ask Tom Lancaster about the money needed for rent." She shrugged. "That's all I can think of."

"Tuesday," he said, "was when she talked to Lancaster for fifteen minutes at a quarter past one in the afternoon."

She made a note on the board. "Tuesday night was the first time my car started honking in the garage for no apparent reason."

"Did the other women talk to you about when the harassing phone calls and stalking started?"

"I'm not exactly sure about the timing. I'll have to check with Franny and the twins. And Sophia—especially Sophia. She's the only one who had contact with Brancusi in Las Vegas."

The first time he met with Franny, she'd stated that she'd been receiving weird phone calls since Wednesday. Moira thought she'd noticed someone following her car on Tuesday night or maybe Wednesday. And Megan clearly remembered a suspicious-looking man watching her and her daughter at the playground on Wednesday.

Accurate reports from the witnesses were important. If Brancusi had been in Las Vegas on Tuesday and Wednesday, he had an alibi.

"Wednesday," he said.

"That's the day Layla was murdered." After she wrote on the whiteboard, she turned to face him. "Has the autopsy been done? Do we have a precise time of death?"

Her question was direct and concise, not emotional. Brooke was managing her sadness without weeping or wailing, but her blue eyes reflected a depth of sorrow, and her voice quavered. Her posture was stiff but not frozen.

When they met for the first time at Franny's house, she'd been on the verge of a panic attack—gasping for breath, twitching, trembling and blushing. As they'd gone deeper and dealt with more horrific aspects of the investigation, she rose to each occasion. Her self-control got stronger and stronger.

"Sometime on Wednesday," he said, "Layla was murdered. Prior to that, we can assume that she was drugged. We don't know exactly where or when this happened or how long she was unconscious. After the murder, lividity showed that her body was on its side, maybe in the trunk of a car."

Brooke swallowed hard. With her left hand, she dashed away a drop of moisture below her eyelid. Had his description been too graphic? She turned away from him, stared at the whiteboard and then pivoted and spun around so quickly that her ponytail bounced. Her actions spoke for themselves: she intended to face the facts. "Her murder and the harassment of the others took place in the same time frame. What does that say about the killer's profile?"

Though she was clearly under stress, her question was smart and appropriate. He'd been debating with himself about how much he should tell her. Carefully watching her blue eyes for signs of panic or any other intense emotion, he talked to her the way he'd speak to any of his colleagues.

"The evidence thus far doesn't point to a sex crime. And the killer wasn't excessively violent." He wasn't saying anything that she didn't already know. "He took care to dress his victim, and her body showed few signs of bruising. He didn't beat or torture her."

"I'm glad for that." Her increased tension was evident but minimal. Her lips thinned. Her left eye blinked and twitched.

"It's possible," he said, "that Layla's murder was an accident."

"Are you saying that he accidentally drugged her? That doesn't make sense."

"He meant to drug her but maybe not to kill her. While she was unconscious, she was under his control. That's part of his motivation. Self-aggrandizement and control."

"Which means he gets a thrill out of frightening somebody like Franny."

"He's aroused, but not necessarily in a sexual way. He might not be important in his everyday life. By taking charge, he has power. Hoping to win your trust, he might offer to help you or to take care of you."

"That sounds like Brancusi," she said. "He kept blabbing about a lucrative business deal."

"Did his documentary actually make much money?"

"I can't give you exact figures, but it was a lot. He sold the piece to a cable network, and there was a book deal. A percentage of his profit went into our joint fund, and we made even more from donations. Lancaster has the figures."

"And you're sure the numbers are accurate."

"Layla reviewed the audits and kept him honest." She frowned. "I guess that will be my job now."

He pointed to the whiteboard. "On Thursday, I responded to Franny's phone call."

"Duly noted." She filled in that blank. "And today is Friday."

Today, the most significant thing they'd discovered, timing-wise, was that Layla's body had been delivered to the cabin between eleven thirty and two—a fact that had not escaped Brooke's notice. As she wrote on the board, she said, "Brancusi drives a van. Transporting Layla to the mountains would have been easy. And he's a film-maker. If he grabbed her from her apartment, he would have known how to disable the cameras in the parking lot."

He moved toward the whiteboard and held it on both sides. "I'll take this to Keller and we can get started with the questions."

"Leave it where it is," she said as she took her phone from her fanny pack. "I'll take a picture and we can transfer it to Keller's phone."

"Good plan."

"I could teach you the basics of using your electronics," she said. "It's crazy for an investigator like you to be wandering around with a spiral notebook in your pocket. Well, maybe not crazy/ psychotic, but definitely annoying."

"Professional opinion?"

"As a certified techie nerd, you bet it is."

BROOKE WALKED BESIDE him through the mostly empty FBI building, an impressive structure that had been completed in 2010 and handled FBI business for Colorado and Wyoming. Past hallways with offices, down a short staircase and through a bullpen area, they took the elevator. When they emerged, he led her into an open area with a fridge and vending machines. On the counter was a microwave, a toaster oven and a coffeemaker.

"Can I get you something to drink?" he asked.

As a rule, she never drank caffeinated beverages after six o'clock. "Herbal tea?"

He fed coins into a machine that offered coffee, decaf and hot water while pointing her toward the selection of tea bags in a case on the counter. Leaving the brewing to her, he made himself a coffee with a pod that brewed one cup at a time.

After her tea had steeped, he asked, "Are you ready?"

"I can handle Icky Nicky Brancusi."

"You and I won't be conducting the interrogation. We'll observe from an adjoining room as Keller asks the questions."

"We'll be behind a two-way mirror." She'd watched enough cop shows on television to know how this worked. "Cool."

"Don't get too excited. These interviews can also be very boring."

Feeling like a superspy, she allowed him to escort her into an office where they met SAC Keller, who, unlike Sloan, was still wearing his necktie. Even at this hour, after midnight, Keller maintained his men-in-black, FBI grooming with a clean-shaven jaw and neatly combed hair. His impeccable white shirt told her that he must have changed when he came back to headquarters.

Though she'd already met him at the cabin, Keller was quick to shake her hand. "Thank you for observing, Ms. Josephson. I appreciate your insights."

"I'll bet you appreciate this timeline even more." She held up her phone to show him. "If you want, I can transfer this image to your phone."

"That would be useful." Instead of giving her his phone, he took hers to perform the transfer of information. Obviously, Keller was more computer-savvy than Sloan. He studied their timeline with interest. "Very useful."

"Will you be interrogating all the suspects at this location?"

"Possibly."

She didn't want to miss her chance to hear what Channing, the nasty little twerp, had to say for himself. "Have you brought in anybody else for questioning?"

Keller glanced past her shoulder to make eye contact with Sloan. "We'll keep you informed."

After providing the very useful timeline, she didn't deserve to be brushed aside. "What about Channing?"

"He's on our radar."

"But you haven't taken him into custody," she said.

"We're doing our job."

When SAC Keller pivoted on his heel and exited the room, she turned to Sloan. "What's his problem? The person who killed Layla set a bomb that could have harmed a lot of other people. It's important to move fast."

"It's not in Keller's nature to share information. I hate to say 'trust me' because of what happened to you when you were a kid, but we're pretty good at what we do. If somebody needs to be in custody, it'll happen."

Was he trying to tell her that Channing was already here, hiding behind one of the many closed doors in the long, empty hallways? Was the peeper, Zachary Doyle, being held in another place? "I want to know everything."

"You've got to be patient. This is one place where you're not the boss, Brooke. We're in charge. That's the FBI culture. I've got to tell you that Keller didn't much care for the idea of allowing you to observe, and it took a firm suggestion from Assistant Director Martinez to make him change his mind."

"I get it. You FBI guys are secretive."

"I could tell you it's for your own protection." He held the door open for her. "But that's not always true."

In a narrow room with dim lights, they met three other agents. Silently, they lined up behind the two-way mirror to watch Keller and Nick Brancusi, who sat at a table facing the mirror. After the basic name, address and time of interview, Keller started at the beginning of their timeline.

"Where were you on Tuesday?"

"Vegas." Brancusi fidgeted in his chair. On the

table in front of him was a half-empty water bottle. He'd peeled off the label. "I can't provide witnesses for every minute of the day, but I played poker from five o'clock in the afternoon to after midnight."

"Wednesday?"

She leaned closer to the glass. Wednesday was the day Layla was murdered. The drive from Denver to Vegas took about twelve hours straight through, but a plane ride was only a couple of hours.

"Still in Vegas," Brancusi said. "I talked to Sophia Rossi in the morning."

"In person or on the phone?" Keller asked. "Keep in mind that we can subpoena your phone records."

Brooke whispered, "That's good. His phone records will show if he called Franny."

Sloan responded, "Unless he used a burner phone."

"In person," Brancusi said. "We met for coffee. By the way, she's in favor of having me do a follow-up documentary on the Hardy Dolls. She's the only one who really appreciated what I did for those girls twelve years ago. She thanked me."

A memory rose from deep inside her. Sometimes the pieces from the past were sounds or music. Other times, a taste would waken a hidden thought. This time, the remembrance was visual. She saw them all as they were twelve years ago.

Skinny and scared, they did their best to keep from crying or complaining as they were filmed on a soundstage or a theater—a place where the lighting could be adjusted.

After the trauma they'd already endured, the court-appointed guardians for the younger girls didn't want them to participate in the film. But they agreed when Lancaster told them about the money that could be made, enough cold hard cash to finance college and set them up for life. To his credit, Lancaster watched over the production like a hawk. There were interviews but no re-enactments.

Brancusi had run a small crew. At that time, the director hadn't bothered with the hipster pose. He typically dressed in a Hawaiian shirt, and his hair was a mass of wild curls already turning gray though he couldn't have been more than forty.

He'd taken a special interest in Sophia. What man wouldn't? She was gorgeous. None of them were ugly, but Sophia was breathtaking. Though barely sixteen, she'd looked like a woman. Of course, Brancusi noticed.

Brooke remembered watching while the film-maker leaned close to whisper in Sophia's ear. She seemed to be enjoying the conversation, gig-gling and making teasing little flicks of her wrists and wiggles of her hips. She moved like a dancer.

Brancusi cupped her breast in his big, ugly hand. He licked his lips as he leaned close for a kiss.

Sophia's eyes went wide. Her fluid movements shut down.

That had been when Brooke flew across the room and barreled into Brancusi. She knocked the man off his feet, leaned over him and spoke in what she hoped was a menacing voice: "Touch her again. And you go to jail."

She turned to Sloan. "He's lying. Sophia would probably talk to him, and she might think a new documentary could help her acting career. But she'd never thank that pedophile."

"What did you call him?"

"Let's just say that there's a reason he liked hanging around with six young women who had been traumatized." Sloan could put that in his profile and smoke it. "I wouldn't be the least tiny bit surprised to find out that he made those harassing phone calls to Franny."

Keller had been making further headway with Brancusi's alibi for Wednesday and Thursday, gathering names and the places Brancusi had been in Vegas. He promised to contact the FBI office in Las Vegas and have them verify the facts.

"Knock yourself out," Brancusi said.

"When did you drive to Denver?"

"I left on Thursday, stopped in Grand Junction for the night and got into town on Friday before noon. That motel in Grand Junction is proof. I paid for it with my credit card."

Keller asked, "What made you decide to come to Denver?"

"I figured that if I could talk to the gals in person, they might change their minds."

"Had you spoken to any of them on the phone?"

"Not exactly, but I've been talking to Tom Lancaster, and he said they might be amenable."

What the hell was Lancaster thinking? Staring through the two-way mirror, Brooke curled her fingers into fists. Why hadn't the lawyer mentioned Brancusi to her?

When Sloan touched her back, she inadvertently flinched. "What?"

"How much longer do you want to stay?" he asked.

If she had been conducting the interrogation, she would have wanted to stay longer and delve deeper. After her crystal-clear memory, she knew Brancusi had been inappropriate with Sophia. And he excelled at manipulating people, tricking them into doing what he wanted. But was he a murderer?

Though she didn't want to let him off the hook, she had to admit that he had a lot of proof for his alibi. He couldn't be in Denver, Grand Junction and Las Vegas at the same time.

She whispered to Sloan, "I don't think we'll learn much more from Brancusi."

"Not likely."

"I don't suppose you know if Peter Channing has been taken into custody."

"No."

She sensed that he was holding back. There was more he could tell her, but she'd need a crowbar to pry it out of him. In his own way, Sloan was almost as secretive as SAC Keller.

She shrugged. "We can leave."

There were things she needed to take care of at home, but she wasn't done with her role in this investigation. Not by a long shot.

Chapter Eleven

After only a few hours of sleep, Sloan drove to Brooke's house the next morning. It was early, before seven o'clock, and he hoped to avoid the circus that would swing into gear as soon as the media figured out Layla's identity and her past. In Colorado, a few horrific crimes had captured the public imagination and stuck in the collective memory: the murder of JonBenét Ramsey, the shooting at Columbine High School and the kidnapping of the Hardy Dolls.

When he turned onto her block, he saw the beginning of chaos. The single police car that had been stationed outside the house to provide protection had been joined by three other DPD vehicles. Uniformed officers were doing their best to control the news trucks and teams of camera operators and TV reporters angling for a shot with Brooke's front door in the background. A news chopper circled overhead.

Nothing about this day was going to be easy. Without leaving his car, Sloan showed his FBI credentials to the cops, dodged around the reporter teams, parked in the driveway and texted Brooke, telling her that he'd arrived.

She texted back, GET IN HERE. NOW.

He strode quickly toward the house, grateful that she opened the door immediately and even more pleased that she slammed it behind him. Noise from the street was audible inside the house, but the mood felt less chaotic. Not that it was calm. Franny and the twins joined Brooke. Four sets of piercing blue eyes stared at him accusingly.

He straightened his necktie. "I wish I could tell you that the killer is in jail."

"But you can't," Megan said. "What am I going to do? I can't hide in Brooke's house forever. Is there any way I can safely take Emily to her soccer practice?"

If he remembered correctly, Megan's daughter was four years old. Skipping a soccer practice didn't seem like a big deal. "We can't guarantee protection at a public park."

Megan stamped her foot. "Emily can't even watch regular TV because there's too much stuff about the Hardy Dolls. She'll have questions."

He realized that Megan hadn't told her daughter about her traumatic past, and he didn't blame her. How could she explain being held captive for several months by a sadist who pretended she was his family? A young kid couldn't be expected to understand, but stories about the Hardy Dolls were going to be hard to avoid. "If you want, I can suggest the name of a child psychologist."

"You can do better than that," Brooke said as she stepped up to his side. "Megan already has a therapist for her daughter. Maybe the FBI can escort her to the house so she can talk to Emily."

When he agreed, she gave him a quick thumbs-up. Brooke played the mother role in this little pack. She cleaned up messes and got things done.

"In the meantime," Moira said as she twirled her long braid between her fingers, "you need to chill, sis. Grab some inner peace. I can show you breathing exercises and yoga poses that'll help you relax."

Megan scoffed. "It'll take more than down-ward-facing dog to make me calmer."

Franny giggled. "I like yoga. Ommmmmm."

"Ommmm." Moira placed her palms together and lowered her head as though praying. "One more time. Ommmm."

"Namaste," Franny said.

"That's enough from you two." Megan turned the spotlight on him again. "I want to hear what Agent Sloan has to say about the investigation."

Sharing information with Brooke was far different from opening up to the whole group. A straightforward, honest conversation might open old wounds and do more harm than good. "Is there coffee?"

"I made it myself," Franny said as she linked her arm through his. "It's really good. I added a pinch of cinnamon and a tiny bit of vanilla bean for flavor."

He'd never been one for fancy coffee, but he didn't want to disappoint this bright-eyed creature who was wearing her crown of roses again. "I'm sure it's delicious."

They trooped into the kitchen and took positions at the large central island. Though there were stools, nobody sat. They were too wired.

Franny handed him a steaming mug of coffee and asked, "Has the FBI arrested Peter Channing yet?"

The directness of her question surprised him. Typically Franny danced around an issue, unable to hold focus. He recalled their conversation from last night and wasn't sure whether she considered Channing to be her hero or a worse villain than Martin Hardy. "He's not in custody."

"Where is he?" Franny's voice held an unmistakable note of fear.

"We're looking for him." Sloan sipped his coffee and shot a glance toward Brooke. Locating Peter Channing was the main reason he'd come to her house, but he couldn't discuss his idea with the rest of the women listening. He needed to get Brooke alone.

She stepped up to the center island and addressed them. "Whether Peter is in custody or not, we have to remember that the killer is still at large. I hired a security team, and our bodyguards will be arriving shortly. Megan and Moira, you each have a guard assigned to you. Franny, you're staying with me, and we'll have one guy at the house. We need to take every precaution, and I mean it. Nobody goes out alone. Don't answer your door. Don't drive yourself."

The other three women nodded.

"These bodyguards," Moira said. "Are they single?"

"I didn't make that a requirement for hiring," Brooke said as she pulled out her phone. "But I have pictures."

She set the phone with the photos on the countertop and stepped back while the other women crowded around, making claims on the bodyguards who were coming to protect them. A healthy response, Sloan thought, though maybe a tiny bit sexist.

It pleased him that Brooke wasn't ogling the bodyguards. She looked pretty today in a black blouse and shorts with her hair brushed to a shine and hanging loose to her shoulders. He pulled her aside. "Can we go somewhere private?"

"I've got just the place."

After telling the others that she'd be back in a minute, she directed him down the stairs to the basement. They passed the door to the shooting range and stopped outside another closed door with a keypad lock.

"What's in here?" he asked.

"Panic room."

BROOKE OPENED THE LOCKS, ushered him inside and closed the reinforced steel door behind them. As soon as the high-tech latch clicked into place, the twenty-two-foot-square room filled with pure, blissful silence. The temperature remained at a constant sixty-five degrees, which was too warm for a wine cellar but energy smart and comfortable enough when she wore the sweater she kept on a hook by the door. She slipped the soft blue cardigan over her black shirt. When she'd designed this room—her favorite place in the house, maybe her favorite place in the whole world— she'd used several different technologies, from bomb shelter to wine cellar to a place to ride out a tornado.

At six feet two inches, Sloan seemed gigantic in the small room, which was crowded by the survival supplies she'd packed inside. He flipped down the double bed that she'd adapted from a railroad Pullman car. "Nice."

"The mattress is fairly decent."

He pointed to the computer screens mounted on the wall by the door that showed views of the interior and exterior of the house. "How do you get electricity in here?"

"Conduits running through the air vents in the ceiling. If I need to close those off, you know, in case somebody tries to drive me out with gas, I have a small battery-powered generator and an oxygen condenser."

Without stretching, he reached up and touched the ceiling. "This room isn't part of the original house."

"I hired a security firm to add three-inch reinforcement to the walls, floor and ceiling. This space is nearly impenetrable."

Being locked in her panic room with him was having an effect on her. He took up a lot of space, and she felt like the walls were closing in…not in a scary way, but intimately wrapping around her, as though she was being squeezed in a gentle embrace. She imagined that she could feel him breathing and hear the steady beat of his heart. No one could find them in here. There would be no interruptions.

Turning away from her, he checked out the stockpile of nonperishable food, water and medical equipment. "You can stay locked up in here for a long time."

"Not really," she said. "If there are two occupants, my supplies won't last more than a week, and that would require rationing. This room isn't meant to be a long-term bomb shelter."

He stood directly in front of her. "What is it meant for?"

"Safety. It's a place to hide."

"From what?"

In light of what had happened to Layla and the media assault taking place on her front lawn, she hardly felt that an explanation was necessary. "Can't you see what it's like? If I let my guard down, I'm exposed. People are always approaching, wanting a hug or to hold my hand or take a selfie. All they really want is to hear the gruesome details."

"Or they might just want to comfort you."

"It's none of their business," she said, more vehemently than intended. The scrutiny reminded her of the past. "I want to be left alone."

"That's not altogether true. You don't mind being with the women upstairs."

"Don't get me wrong, I love Franny and the twins. But sometimes they make me crazy. Always calling or showing up on the doorstep, wanting me to help them. You saw how nervous Franny got when she couldn't reach Layla on the phone."

"As it turned out," he said, "her fears were justified."

"Let's call that another really good reason for me to have a panic room."

He engaged her with a smile. "You make me think of those tricky little bunny rabbits that set up several hidey-holes they can duck into to evade their enemies. You have this room and the cabin that you and Layla had in the mountains. Anywhere else?"

"If I told you, it wouldn't be a hidey-hole, would it?"

"No need to worry about me. I'm not a predator."

When she gazed into his breathtaking gray eyes, she saw an edge of danger. *Watch out for him!* Not that Sloan would physically harm her, but he had the power to tantalize and mesmerize until she let her guard down. She didn't want to be vulnerable. "There's nothing wrong with taking precautions."

"You're right. The world is a dangerous place. It's smart to be vigilant. As for this panic room, well, I've got to tell you that I love it. If this hideout was mine, I'd be in here all the time. It's like a secret fortress."

"You sound like a kid. Did you have a clubhouse when you were growing up?"

"Me and my brother built a tree house. We had a bunch of comic books, baseball cards, candy and toys. And binoculars. We could see over the fence into the neighbor's yard."

She wished her childhood held such pleasant memories. Brooke had never really been a kid. She'd grown up too soon. "I was a loner, the kind of kid who sits by herself in the lunchroom. That might be why Hardy selected me. Even someone like him could see that I wouldn't be missed."

"But you weren't shy. You were the leader."

"Not right away. At first, my job was to clean and make sure everybody got fed. Then, they started calling me 'Mama,' and I grew into that role. What a joke!" The irony pained her, and she talked fast to cover the ache in her heart. "I didn't know what a mother should be. My birth mom was gone before I even knew her name."

"According to your records, you were adopted as an infant."

"By the Josephson family." She had a photo of them holding her at a baptism. "They named me Brooke because my eyes were as blue as a mountain stream. They seemed like nice people, and I wish I could remember them. Mrs. Josephson passed away from cancer when I was four, and Mister couldn't take care of me. After that, it was welcome to foster care."

"When you were four?"

"And I wasn't a cutie-pie. Mr. Josephson didn't know how to feed me or keep me clean. My hair was chopped short, and the kids at the first home teased me about looking like a boy. One of them called me a scrawny mongrel."

"Not a happy memory."

"I didn't know what the words meant. I remembered them so I could find out." She didn't usually talk so much about herself. "Tell me about you."

"There's nothing too exciting. I grew up in the

burbs outside Chicago, did okay in school, went into the navy and ended up at Quantico for FBI training."

"There's something more." Without touching him, she scooted around the room and sat on the edge of the Murphy bed. She wrapped her sweater more tightly around her. "Your life hasn't been all sunshine. I've seen glimpses of a shadow."

"A shadow, huh?" He sat beside her. "You sound like Moira."

"Oh, I hope not. I can't keep up with her yoga and Wicca and chanting."

"This room makes you feel safe," he said. "Are there people who reassure you in the same way? Maybe Gimbel?"

Though she noticed that Sloan had cleverly deflected her inquiry into his personal life, she didn't push. His question intrigued her. Who made her feel safe? "I trust Gimbel, but I wouldn't expect him to have my back in a moment of danger. He's not as energetic as he used to be, and I'm probably a better shot."

"To feel safe, you need to be with someone who can physically protect you."

"I do." She looked down at her hands in her lap. "There are plenty of people who are supportive of me, like Franny, Sophia and the twins. And I have a therapist, Dr. Joan, who I can tell anything. But when I'm scared, really scared, I need muscles—somebody who's kick-ass."

"Not what I was expecting to hear."

"I kind of surprised myself," she said. "I don't want you to think that I'm a dopey damsel in distress who needs to be rescued."

"I would never think of you as helpless."

"I'm a little bit kick-ass myself."

"More than a little bit."

She shifted position but didn't put more distance between them. Being close to him, alone with him, was surprisingly comfy. Never before had she felt so warm and cozy in this room. She looked down at his right hand resting on the bed between them. Acting on impulse, she glided her fingers across his knuckles.

As soon as she touched him, he reacted. Nothing obvious, just a twitch, but it was enough to cause her to look up. She studied his lips, his cheekbones and his clean-shaven jaw, looking for a reason why he appealed to her. His features projected masculinity. Sloan was strong enough to fight off any predator. He could keep her safe. *At what cost?* The shimmer from his fascinating gray-green eyes enticed her. Did she feel safe with him? Definitely, she felt something. Her sensation of cozy warmth turned to excitement. Her vision blurred around the edges. Her heart thumped, and butterflies did pirouettes in her stomach.

Somehow, they were holding hands. She swallowed hard. *What does this mean?* They were alone, sitting on the bed in her panic room. Instead of overthinking and considering every alternative, she leaned toward him. They kissed.

Sensations cascaded through her body. She was confused but delighted. How could she be shivering and sweating at the same time? Neon lights flared behind her closed eyelids. Her rigid grasp on self-control relaxed, and she was amazed.

His lips parted. He probed with his tongue, and she opened her mouth to draw him inside. Gentle at first, he teased her with his passion, and she returned the favor, tasting the slick surface of his teeth and pressing her mouth hard against his, kissing him ravenously. She heard someone moaning. *Oh, it's me.*

Their physical contact broke the rules. He was an FBI agent and, therefore, could get into big trouble for this indiscretion. She ought to make him stop.

But it was Sloan who ended the kiss. "Are you okay?"

So much better than okay—she'd caught a hint of what sex ought to be about. Her prior experiences were obviously mistakes. "You said you wanted to be alone with me. Is this the reason why?"

"I'm glad we went down this road," he said.

"Me, too."

"But it's not the reason I wanted a private moment. We have a problem with Peter Channing."

His words fell with heavy thuds. With reluctance, she rose from the bed and returned to the real world.

Chapter Twelve

Given a choice, Sloan would have kept the reinforced steel door to the panic room locked and put that pull-down bed to good use. Brooke's kiss surprised him, even though he'd been imagining her as his lover from the first moment they met. Maybe it wasn't the first moment, when she blasted him with the pepper spray, but shortly thereafter. He'd been intrigued.

Who was this lady? Brooke was beautiful, with her soft lips, creamy complexion and shiny black hair curling around the perfect oval of her face. Also, she was sexy. Her kiss had started as a tentative taste but quickly jump-started a whole different level of arousal. An incredible woman, she was smart, brave and had a sense of humor. He even liked the way she focused on being well organized, probably because he had a few OCD issues of his own. He liked rules and preferred to have things neat and tidy, which made the proposal he was about to suggest more difficult. He watched her pace in a very small circle.

"What about Channing?" she asked. "You said you hadn't located him."

"We have a phone number, address, license plate number and all the other basic data. But we haven't been able to make contact."

"What about the girlfriend, the woman he's supposed to marry?" she asked. "He could be staying with her."

"One of our agents went to her place. She said she hadn't seen Channing since he went to work at about nine o'clock yesterday. Before that, he'd been with her."

"Where does he work?"

"A food truck called Taco Guac. Our agent talked to the guys who worked there yesterday. They said the truck was parked in Civic Center from ten o'clock to two, and Channing was there the whole time. According to our timeline, that gives him an alibi." They'd figured that the murderer had brought Layla's body to the cabin between eleven thirty and two. "He's in the clear, unless the Taco Guac guys are lying."

Her nervous pacing came to an abrupt halt as she pulled off her blue sweater and tossed it onto a hook by the door. Her flushed cheeks emphasized the blue of her eyes as she stared at him. "Why would the Guac guys lie?"

"He could have paid them off. They could be

good buddies. Or they might just hate the FBI. You'd be shocked by how many people lie to us."

Her eyebrows arched. "I hope you're being sarcastic."

"Yeah, I am. In the old days, the FBI got more respect than now," he said. "Anyway, Channing won't answer his phone and hasn't gone back to his apartment."

"But that doesn't make sense," she said. "If he's not the killer, why would he go on the run? What does he have to hide?"

"We need to interrogate him. His emails to Layla must have some significance." After he'd handed over the thumb drive, Keller had wasted no time picking out the emails and printing them. The contents seemed innocent enough. Channing was reaching out to Layla, telling her about his upcoming wedding and hinting that he'd like to see her. The person he really wanted to meet again was Franny. "Did you read them?"

She nodded. "He referred to us as his sisters and said that he missed us. When he was playing with us at the cabin, he somehow didn't notice the chains on our ankles and didn't hear Franny sobbing after his uncle mutilated her finger. Was he so desperately lonely that he actually thought we were his family?"

"It's possible."

"I don't know whether to hate him or pity him."

"His life must have gotten worse after his uncle was convicted and sent away to a federal prison. Channing was part of a notorious family, probably shunned by the other kids."

She wrapped her arms around her middle, looked down for a long moment and frowned. "Nope, I don't feel sorry for him. He could have helped us escape."

Sloan had to agree with her. As a trained psychologist, he could dredge up a raggedy chunk of empathy for Channing, but the kid had been eleven at the time, and that was old enough to know right from wrong. He'd enjoyed his trips to the cabin too much—probably had a sadistic streak. Still, his behavior didn't fit the profile for a killer.

His emails to Layla were polite and friendly. As Brooke pointed out, his memories were delusional. But he wasn't lewd or hostile. It was hard to imagine him making threatening phone calls to Franny, whom he genuinely liked. If he'd managed to reach his favorite girl from long ago, he would have invited her to a movie. In his mind, they were friends.

"He doesn't have a rap sheet," he said. "A couple of speeding tickets, but that's all. He never went to college. Mostly, he's been working in restaurants and has been employed by Taco Guac for six months."

She sank down on the bed beside him. "It doesn't seem like Channing is the killer."

"But I still need to talk to him. Layla's murder has too many connections to the past to ignore. Channing might refer us to someone else." He turned his head toward her. "That's where you come in."

"I'll do whatever it takes to help."

"Channing hasn't gone back to his apartment, and his phone is turned off, so we can't trace him. He's not answering messages from the FBI, but he'd probably listen if the call came from you."

"Seriously?" Her eyes popped wide. "You want me to call the twerp?"

"Maybe don't start by calling him names."

"Twerp is exactly right," she said. "That was my nickname for him."

"You'd send him a message on a throwaway phone, assure him that everything is okay and tell him to call you back. When he responds, you set up a meeting. Not with you, but with me."

"This plan sounds flaky to me. Has Keller signed off on it?"

"Surprisingly, he has. We're having no luck with Channing, and it's making Keller furious. He's willing to bend the rules if it means getting this investigation moving. It's a high-profile case. If he solves it, he looks good."

She held out her hand. "Give me the phone. I'll leave a message and send a text."

He took a cell phone from his jacket pocket. "Do you get reception down here?"

"It's specially wired. I don't want to get trapped in my panic room with no way to contact the outside world."

"Before you make the phone call, take a breath. Your voice needs to sound welcoming, not threatening."

"Got it." After he punched in the number, she held the phone while it rang and went to voice mail. She cleared her throat and talked to the phone. "Hello, twerp. It's me, Brooke. I want to talk. Call me back on this number."

She tapped a text message in a similar tone, and then handed him the phone. "Now what?"

"Now we wait," he said.

BROOKE LED SLOAN from the panic room to the kitchen, where they rejoined the others. They were just in time to greet the three bodyguards, who were—as their photos promised—muscular, well-groomed and studly. These guys would give Sloan a run for his money, but she still thought the FBI special agent had the bodyguards beat, even though he was wearing a sedate dark gray suit and they were dressed in three different versions of cargo pants and form-hugging T-shirts. She supposed they were trying to look casual, as if these guys could blend in with the crowd.

Sloan kept the cell phone in his possession. As

soon as it rang or got a response to her text, they'd go down the hall to her office for the conversation with Channing. Since he was no longer a viable suspect, her attitude toward the twerp had mellowed. She hadn't forgiven him and never would. But she didn't despise him.

Though she was happily married, Megan flirted with enthusiasm as little Emily linked hands with the bodyguard assigned to them and pulled him toward the upstairs bedroom where she'd been playing with coloring books. When they left the kitchen, Megan gave Brooke a wink. "If I take him with us to soccer practice, I'll be the most popular mom on the field."

Brooke didn't want her to be scared, but she didn't want her to be stupid, either. "He's a bodyguard, not an accessory. You need to follow his rules to stay safe."

"I'm sure I won't mind having him tell me exactly what to do."

Moira consulted a computer program with an astrological ephemeris to make sure that she and her assigned guard were compatible. Franny chatted cheerfully with her bodyguard, who was her new best friend.

Sloan took a position beside Brooke at the kitchen island. "You seem to have everything under control."

"It's what I do."

When there was another knock at the door,

the bodyguard assigned to her house checked the camera surveillance and held the computer tablet so she could see. One of the cops had escorted Tom Lancaster to her doorstep. He was more formal than usual, wearing a suit and carrying an attaché. He probably wanted to impress the media.

Brooke gave the security code to the bodyguard and told him to open the door. Though she wasn't real happy with Lancaster for having a chat with Icky Nicky Brancusi, she was relieved that he was here. Layla's death would generate a lot of paperwork, and—since she had no family—the arrangements would be Brooke's responsibility. She knew what Layla wanted—one night, they'd shared a bottle of wine and their conversation turned morbid. They'd talked about what they wanted for their funerals. Both preferred cremation. Layla had specifically said she didn't want a gravestone and hoped her ashes could be scattered in the mountains near their cabin.

Not there. That cabin was where the killer left her body. Even in the supposed safety of their hideaway, their past had found them. The irony enraged her. Brooke found herself gripping Sloan's hand and squeezing his fingers hard.

Quietly, he murmured, "Are you okay?"

"I'll be fine."

When Lancaster entered, he greeted one of the bodyguards by name and told him that he was glad Brooke had gone with his firm, which was the one he'd recommended. He turned to Brooke and said, "We have paperwork and other details to work through. Maybe we should go to your office."

"Of course." She didn't make the mistake of thinking that Lancaster was being sensitive to the feelings of the other women and trying to avoid upsetting them with talk of Layla's death. The lawyer had worked with them long enough to know that they wouldn't get business done in a group setting. He was being efficient.

In her office, she took the chair behind the desk, the power position. Lancaster stood on the opposite side, and Sloan was by the door. He checked the burner phone she'd used to call Channing and put it back into his pocket. She hoped the twerp would contact her soon. Thus far, the investigation had gone from one dead end to another. They desperately needed some kind of direction.

Before Lancaster took a seat, he scowled at Sloan and muttered an unintelligible comment under his breath. Brooke knew they'd argued last night. "Gentlemen, is there a problem?"

"This is confidential information," the lawyer said. "We don't need him."

"Special Agent Sloan and I are working together on the investigation," she said. "Anything you say to me, you can say to him."

"You? You're playing detective for the FBI?"

"I'm a consultant."

"I don't approve. It's dangerous."

"And it's my decision."

What gave him the right to tell her what to do? Sloan had characterized Lancaster as a narcissist. Though she'd never really thought about it before, she had to agree. In her transcription work, she frequently came into contact with lawyers and doctors. Many of them had egos as vast as Montana. It was no surprise that Lancaster fit that profile.

"We'll get started," he said as he placed his attaché on the desktop and opened it. "As soon as I have official copies of the death certificate, I'll deal with Layla's creditors, debts and insurance policies. The deed for the cabin should be transferred to your name only."

"I'm not sure I want to keep it," she said. "I wasn't aware that there were insurance policies."

"One she got through the college and another for student loans. There might be more. She kept me up-to-date on her business dealings, but I'm not sure I have everything. The explosion destroyed a lot of information."

She glanced toward Sloan. "I believe the FBI has accessed the data on her personal computer, which I would have grabbed off her desk if I'd been thinking properly."

"We were right to run," Sloan said. "The computer was plugged in to other devices, and we would have wasted precious minutes disconnecting. As it was, we barely escaped in time."

"What a mess!" Lancaster shook his bald head in disbelief. "Why on earth would the killer blow up her office?"

"To hide something," she said.

"How did you know the bomb was in the office?" Sloan asked.

"Must have heard it on the news. And Brooke just mentioned the desk."

She wasn't exactly sure what was going on with these two men. Either Sloan was suspicious of Lancaster or he really didn't like the lawyer... or a bit of both.

"Anyway," she said, "when we first came into her apartment, I could tell that it had been searched. Layla must have had evidence that pointed to the identity of the killer. And when he couldn't find it..."

"He blew the place up," Lancaster said, "to cover his tracks."

That theory made as much sense as anything else. Maybe Channing had placed the bomb to hide his correspondence with Layla, but she didn't think the twerp was clever enough to rig a specialized trigger. Not to mention that he had a fairly good alibi. Who could have set a bomb? "The explosive device was sophisticated."

"Something like that can be bought." Lancaster tilted his head back and looked down his nose at Sloan. "Does the FBI have any leads about the bomber?"

"No arrests have been made."

She appreciated his noncommittal attitude. He wasn't spilling information but wasn't being rude to her lawyer.

Lancaster took a typed sheet of paper from a file folder inside his briefcase and placed it on the desk in front of her. "This is the first draft of the obituary. You'll need to add details about the funeral home, memorial services and where people should send flowers."

"Cremation. No burial. No flowers. Layla did pro bono work for a homeless shelter and for foster kids. Those would be good places for donations. As for a memorial? I don't know."

She hated the idea of weeping mourners who had never known her friend. At the same time, she understood how people were touched by Layla's story and needed to express their grief. Memorials were supposed to give closure, but she wasn't so sure. Before she presented the plan to the others, she wanted to talk it over with someone…with Sloan. He'd listen and give good advice.

"A suggestion," Lancaster said. "Since we already have the fund set up and ready to accept donations, we could ask people to send money there. Later, we'll disperse various amounts to Layla's favorite causes."

"I'd rather start a different fund using her name. She had a separate life that wasn't part of our combined tragedy. She was special."

"Okay, okay, consider it done. What about Layla's will? We ought to set an appointment for the reading."

"No need to rush," she said, "unless there's a time-sensitive issue."

"Not really, but—"

"I have to interrupt," Sloan said. "Brooke has a text that needs to be answered right away."

Excitement rushed through her. Channing was returning her message. Their plan was working. She bounded to her feet. "We're done here, Mr. Lancaster. Please leave."

The lawyer shuffled to his feet and grumbled, moving slowly until Sloan grabbed his attaché, snapped the latch and tossed it into the hallway. Grumbling louder, the lawyer followed his paperwork out the door.

When they were alone, Sloan showed her the screen on the burner phone with the text message from Peter Channing. Not a twerp. Call in five minutes. Use this number.

Though she'd been hoping for a contact, a shiver of apprehension went through her. "What should I do?"

"Have you ever seen that phone number before?"

"I don't think so."

"He must have picked up a burner phone of his own. Maybe he's not as dumb as we thought. The FBI is monitoring the number that belongs to him and can use it to track his location." He came around the desk and stood in front of her. "Put the phone on speaker and call the twerp."

"What do I say?"

"Set up a meeting for me. Tell him he's not in trouble, and I just want to talk. Whatever you do, don't make promises you can't keep—don't get yourself involved." He placed the phone on the desk and turned his attention back to her. Gently, he grasped her upper arms and made eye contact. "You can handle this."

She wished for a ton more confidence. "What if he refuses?"

"You'll convince him. He'll listen to you. They all listen to you." He guided her to the desk chair and got her seated. "You're the boss."

She reminded herself that the twerp probably wasn't the killer. Could she be certain of that? Was it possible for Channing to have killed Layla? If she arranged a meeting, would she be sending Sloan into a trap?

She punched in the numbers. The phone rang twice before a man's voice answered, "Hi, Brooke. Long time, no see."

He didn't sound at all like the preadolescent kid who'd come to the cabin and played with Franny.

He was a grown man, twenty-three years old. "I could say the same to you."

"I'm sorry, like, really sorry, about what happened to Layla. She was always nice to me. Not like you. Layla never, ever called me a twerp."

He had the deep voice of an adult, but his words were childish. She could have been talking to an eleven-year-old, chastising him for tracking mud into the cabin. "I'm helping the FBI investigate. They want to talk to you."

"No way. I won't let them arrest me. I won't. This isn't my fault. I didn't do anything wrong. You can't trick me, Brooke. Not like when I was a kid. I know what the FBI is after. They want to lock me up and throw away the key."

"They only want information. You're not a suspect."

"I don't believe you. Damn, Brooke, you don't know what it was like after Uncle Martin got arrested. When people heard my name, they'd run away. I didn't have any friends. All I wanted was to talk to Franny. I missed her so much. She was my best little buddy. Do you know how I can find her?"

His tirade worried her. She'd never tell him how to reach Franny, and she needed to change the subject. "Things are better for you now. You have a girlfriend. You're going to get married."

"So what?"

"You have a happy, decent life ahead of you.

All you need to do is talk to this one FBI agent and get it over with."

There was a long pause. She looked up at Sloan. He gave her an encouraging grin.

"Peter, are you there?"

"Ten minutes from right now. Tell him to go to Molly May's Café on Colfax and sit in one of the booths by the front window."

Success! "Thanks, Peter."

"There's one more thing, Brooke. You need to come with the FBI guy. If you're not sitting in the booth at the window where I can see you, I won't come inside."

How could she say no? Peter Channing could play cat-and-mouse games with the FBI for days while the evidence evaporated and the leads turned icy cold. "I'll be there."

"Good."

"Now I have a question for you. Molly May's is close to my house. How did you know I could get there in ten minutes?"

"Check your local news. They're broadcasting from your front yard, and I've been watching since six o'clock this morning. See you in ten, Brooke."

Her heart stopped. He'd been watching? She swiveled in her desk chair and stared through the window at the backyard. Was Channing out there? Hiding behind the tall, cedar privacy fence or lurking in shadow of a big-leafed catalpa tree?

Her house—her sanctuary—was being broadcast on television sets all over Denver. She might never feel safe again.

Chapter Thirteen

Brooke expected Sloan to be annoyed with her. She'd disregarded his instruction about not getting involved. When Channing said she had to attend the meeting, she'd been quick to agree. Not a single attempt at negotiating. No objections, none at all.

Rationalizing, she told herself that she hadn't wanted to scare him off. The twerp might have details about Layla's death, and they needed all the information they could get. "I didn't have a choice," she said.

"No, you did not."

Whew! "I guess I'm coming with you."

"Much as I'd rather have you tucked away in your panic room with a bodyguard keeping watch, you made a promise. If you're not there, Channing will take off like a white-tailed jackrabbit. He shouldn't be a problem. I don't believe this guy poses much of a threat."

"Me neither." Talking to him hadn't scared her. The thought of him sneaking around and peeping into her house made her uneasy but not panicked. If she'd spotted him, she wouldn't have hesitated to pull her Glock from her desk drawer and take aim.

"The way I figure," Sloan said, "if he wanted to hurt you, he would have chosen a more clandestine spot than Molly May's Café."

"Let me grab my fanny pack, and we'll go."

"We're going to need help from the cops on duty to get past the media. Do what I say, move fast and don't tell the others where we're headed."

She strapped on her fanny pack. "Should I take my gun?"

"No."

He ushered her through the house, made excuses for why they needed to rush and promised to be back soon. Megan pressed a "while you're out" shopping list into her hand. And Franny gave her a hug.

After a speedy switcheroo with the cops, they were in his SUV, headed toward Molly May's, a cute little café with plastic daisies on the tables and gingham curtains. Though the checkered pattern was red, it reminded her of the apron she had to wear at the cabin. They sat at one of the three booths by the front window. Because they were side by side instead of opposite each other, she rearranged the silverware so they each had their separate knife, fork and spoon at their right hand. A waitress in a white uniform with an apron that matched the curtains served coffee. If she spilled, would she be forced to scrub at the stain until her fingers were raw? Had Channing known about the gingham?

Brooke looked down at her hands in her lap and realized that she'd shredded her paper napkin. Squeezing the tattered napkin into a ball, she looked out the window, watching the sidewalk and the cars on Colfax—a long, straight street that always had traffic, even at ten o'clock on a Saturday.

In spite of Sloan's assurance that they were in no danger, she noticed that he'd positioned himself so his right side was free. He had easy access to his handgun.

"Do you see him?" he asked.

"I'm not sure I'd recognize him if I did."

As she watched a red truck slow down as it passed the café, her tension level ratcheted up higher. What if he didn't show? *What would she do when he did?* A couple of other cars cruised slowly with the drivers watching. Then she saw a guy shuffling along the sidewalk. A backward Bronco cap covered his close-cropped hair, and his baggy brown shorts flapped around his skinny legs. His posture was dreadful. His feet seemed too big for the rest of him. She wasn't surprised when he waved.

"That's him." Waving back, she felt her mouth curling into a smile. *Why?* Channing was part of her captivity, complicit with his uncle. She ought to hate him.

He picked his way through the café, twice bumping into chairs, and joined them at their table. A dopey grin spread across his face, and she squeezed her lips together so she wouldn't smile back at him.

"Stop staring, Peter. It's rude."

He chuckled. "You're still trying to boss everybody around."

"Allow me to introduce Special Agent Sloan, and then sit down."

After the two men shook hands, Channing scooted into the booth opposite her and Sloan. Like his big feet, his overlarge hands dangled from bony wrists. She noticed several scars from burns and cuts that must have come from his work in the food truck. Considering how clumsy he was walking through a mostly vacant restaurant, she expected worse.

"Do you like working at Taco Guac?" she asked.

"Yep." His head bobbed. "Did you recognize me right away?"

"I knew it was you when I saw—" she pointed to the corner of her mouth "—your dimple. Do you still have the scar on your leg?"

"You bet." He started to hoist his leg onto the table. "Want to see?"

"I'll take your word."

"I would have known you anywhere, Brooke.

You're so pretty. All you dolls were pretty, especially Franny. I think about her all the time. Should I invite her to my wedding? Would she come?"

"I can't speak for Franny." His expression was open, innocent and alarmingly immature. Channing had a man's body but acted like a little boy. How could he forget that when he knew them, they were prisoners? Shackled to their beds, brutalized by his uncle, they weren't his cheerful playmates. She didn't want to bond with him, and she sure as hell wouldn't put him in touch with Franny.

"I tried to get ahold of you and the other dolls. Just to talk, but no. No way. You were hiding behind unlisted phone numbers and computer firewalls and secret addresses. There were restraining orders."

"But you managed to send Layla a couple of emails. How did that happen?"

"She's a new lawyer, looking for business. Her email address was on a flyer for a homeless shelter."

"Pro bono." Her services were free to people who were down on their luck. Layla wanted to help. Instead, she'd attracted Channing, which was a perfect example of how no good deed went unpunished.

"It's cool that she's a lawyer." He wiped a hand

over his face to erase his grin. "I'm sorry about what happened to her, really sorry."

Sloan cleared his throat. "I have a few questions."

"First, let me order."

Channing waved the waitress over to their table. It was a few minutes after ten o'clock, early enough for breakfast. He ordered waffles and bacon. Sloan did the same. Brooke didn't want food. Her easygoing chat with Channing wasn't sitting well in her stomach.

While she sipped her coffee, Sloan ran through Channing's whereabouts for the week. He worked every day and spent most of his downtime with his fiancée, but there were gaps in his activities on Wednesday and Thursday when he could have met with Layla. Yesterday's alibi for eleven thirty until two gave him an out.

The longer they talked, the less she believed he was the killer. Channing was too clumsy to have performed the surgical search at Layla's apartment. He didn't have the smarts to build a bomb or the money to hire someone else to do it.

After their food was served, she asked, "Why were you avoiding the FBI?"

"I've had bad experiences with cops. No offense, Sloan."

"None taken," Sloan said as he drenched his waffles with syrup. "What kind of bad experience?"

"As soon as they figure out who I am and how

I was connected to the dolls, they get mean. They slap me around, zap me with Tasers and call me a pedophile. It wasn't my fault. I tried to help, but I was only eleven."

"Old enough to know right from wrong," she said. There was a limited amount of time that she could hold back her resentment.

"Don't start." He shoveled a forkful of waffles into his mouth, chewed fast and swallowed with a gulp. He vacuumed up another bite. Preparing fast food on a truck had apparently turned him into a speedy eater. "I've got to tell you, Brooke, you didn't make things easy?"

"Seriously? You're blaming me for your problems?"

"You hurt me." She heard a disturbing edge in his voice and reminded herself that just because he appeared boyish, he could still be dangerous. "You and Franny. You hurt my feelings."

"I don't believe you."

"You were a mean girl. You had all these rules about keeping quiet and not making a mess. I always tried to bring food with me. Don't you remember the jars of peanut butter? My girlfriend says I was trying to buy your love."

She glanced toward Sloan. "Does this make sense to you?"

He gave a brief nod.

As if she should feel responsible for any way that Channing had messed up his life? He wasn't her responsibility. "Your uncle never should have brought you to the cabin."

"But he did, and I wanted to be nice to you. After Halloween, I gave the dolls all my candy. At least Franny was happy."

"Stop saying *dolls*," she said.

"But that's what everybody calls you." His narrow shoulders rose and fell in a shrug. For a few minutes, he ate. The food on his plate disappeared at a startling rate. "You always were touchy and bossy. You had secrets."

Sloan asked, "What kind of secrets?"

"She was like the magpies I saw on a nature show. They're always hopping around, stealing shiny things and tucking them away in secret nests."

Sloan glanced down at her. His unspoken message was clear. She still had secrets and hiding places. So what if that was true? She had nothing to feel bad about.

Channing continued, "One time, she took nail clippers from my uncle and when he noticed and got mad, she pretended like she'd just found them so nobody would get punished."

These sad, pathetic memories disgusted her. She'd started with stealing loose change from Hardy, thinking that she'd have enough to buy her way to freedom—a plan that made no sense whatsoever. Who did she intend to pay? "I did what I had to do to survive."

"Do you remember when I gave you the key?"

A wave of guilt splashed over her, and she covered her feelings by taking a long sip from her nearly empty coffee cup. Though she wished she could forget, the memory was horrible and clear. She hadn't known how long they'd been at the cabin because there was no good way to keep track, but the weather was warmer, almost like spring. Channing had come through with a useful gift. He regularly brought trinkets for Franny, but this was for her: a key that would unlock the metal shackle fastened to her ankle.

Channing had whispered that he needed the key back before he left, and he'd told her to do what she needed to do. She could have escaped but had been paralyzed by fear. What if Hardy caught her? She'd already seen him cut off the tip of Franny's finger. He regularly raped Layla. She'd felt the force of his wrath when he beat her. Did she dare to run? Where would she go?

Sitting in a booth at Molly May's, she shuddered. A painful heat rose from her belly and spread through her body. She was sweating. Her throat felt dry. Some wounds never healed. She was crazy to think she could make this better.

Her captivity had been more than physical. Hardy had imprisoned her soul. She'd been afraid to use the key, terrified of the consequences. Everybody, including Sloan, thought she was brave, but they were wrong. She was a coward who didn't deserve to be in charge. Because she was too scared to act, they'd been in captivity for two more months, Layla had been raped many more times, and Sophia, too. Brooke had let them down. And it was happening again. Layla's killer was outsmarting her. She wasn't smart or courageous enough to stop him. He was getting away with his heinous crimes.

Her insights provided no help at all. It was time for her to step away before she messed up this investigation.

Channing and Sloan continued talking while they finished their breakfast. The twerp apologized for avoiding the cops and took Sloan's business card, promising to call him if anything else occurred to him. All in all, he wasn't a bad kid. It wasn't his fault that his uncle was a monster.

When they left the booth, Channing tried to give her a hug. *Not yet.* She wasn't ready to forgive him, but she kept smiling. "This wasn't too bad," she said.

"Same to you."

Sloan paid, and they followed Channing out the door, where they saw Brancusi step out from behind a dark brown van with a gold stripe on the side. He held a small camera to his eye and was videotaping them.

"Don't pay any attention to me," he said. "Keep doing what you were doing."

"Who the hell is this guy?" Channing demanded.

Sloan stalked toward the filmmaker and held the flat of his hand in front of the lens. "You don't have permission to film us."

"A technicality." Brancusi lowered the camera and called to Channing, "Hey, kid, do you want to make a couple hundred bucks?"

Though his eyes lit up at the mention of easy money, he shook his head. "You stay away from me."

"Your fiancée was more cooperative," Brancusi said with a sleazy leer. "A whole lot more cooperative."

Channing charged the few yards across the asphalt parking lot and lunged at Brancusi, who pivoted to protect his camera equipment. It wouldn't be a fair confrontation. Channing had youth on his side, but the documentarian had experience. Though Brancusi dressed like a bearded hipster, he moved like a street fighter. Darting back to the driver's side of his van, he whipped open the door and emerged with a tire iron.

Sloan drew his weapon and aimed. "Put it down."

"He started it," Brancusi said. "He came at me."

"If you disarm yourself, get in your van and drive away, I won't arrest you," Sloan said. "Do us all a favor—don't be an ass."

The threat of being arrested made a difference. Brancusi backed off. Before he closed the door to his van, he said, "Here's a favor for you, Sloan. If you want to solve this, meet with the kid's fiancée."

Dismissively, Sloan turned away from him and spoke to Channing. "Are you okay?"

"I don't like that guy."

"Nobody does," Brooke said.

He gave her a dimpled grin and checked his wristwatch. "If I hustle, I can make my shift at Taco Guac. Call me if there's anything I can do to help."

"I will." Maybe she would.

"And tell Franny to give me a call. Any time."

She watched him walk to the end of the parking lot and climb into his car. Seeing Channing hadn't been what she expected. She'd thought she'd be hostile toward him. Instead, her anger and tension came from inside. Her head ached with memories of her mistakes and bad decisions. The guilt crushed her spirit. She had no business being involved in the investigation. She should step aside and let the FBI do their job.

"I'm done," she said. "Take me back to the house."

"So far, the guy who best fits the profile for a murderer is Brancusi," Sloan said as he walked her back to his SUV and opened the passenger-side door for her. "The filmmaker is a typical sociopath."

"What does that mean?"

"His grasp on right and wrong is tenuous. His morality is based on self-interest. Whatever's right for him is the course he chooses."

"That sounds like a lot of businessmen I've known."

"Sociopaths can be very successful. They're capable of being charming when it suits them, but they have almost zero empathy. I can easily imagine Brancusi making cruel phone calls to Franny, not caring that he hurt her."

"Is that the profile for a killer?"

"It could be."

His information tantalized her. Psychology was interesting, and sometimes her sessions with Dr. Joan helped…but not right now. The clearer her memories got, the worse she felt about herself. She needed to go home and clean out a drawer or straighten the dishes in the kitchen. In this situation, she was blinded by emotion. Her intelligence was worthless. There was no way she could help solve this murder. She should bow out now.

She climbed into the SUV and fastened her seat belt. "It sounds like you've got it all figured out."

"I haven't." He went around to the driver's side and slid behind the steering wheel. "Brancusi has an alibi. He was in Las Vegas when the murder took place. Do you think he was working with somebody else?"

She shook her head. "You should be talking to somebody who understands these things."

"I want your insights and your help." He fired up the engine. "What's going on, Brooke? You're not a quitter."

"How do you know? We've only been together a couple of days."

"I know you'll do anything to catch Layla's murderer."

Dammit, he was right. "Fine. What do we do next?"

"Follow up on a clue from Brancusi. While Channing is at work on the food truck, we're going to pay a visit to his fiancée."

Chapter Fourteen

Sloan's job was to profile and apprehend the killer, but he had other motivations. Right now, he was worried about Brooke. The memories triggered by her conversation with Channing must have been dark and heavy. It wasn't the mention of secret hidey-holes that upset her. She was aware of that glitch in her personality. When they were alone in her panic room, she'd admitted to a penchant for secret stashes and hiding places.

He'd noticed a different reaction when Channing recalled a specific incident involving a key. The symbolism of a key, especially to someone who was being held captive, was huge. Had he thwarted her escape? Was she unable to flee when offered an opportunity? Later, they'd talk about it. First, he needed to assess her behavior and decide if she'd be able to help as they moved forward.

"I hope you'll stay with the investigation." He checked the address for Channing's girlfriend in his spiral notebook before he drove the SUV through the parking lot beside Molly May's and exited onto Colfax Avenue. "If you've changed your mind and don't want to be involved, I'll understand."

"I doubt that."

"Give me a break. I understand a lot."

"Do you really?"

She wasn't ready to be open, but he heard a shift in her tone of voice. The darkness might be receding. "You're not a total woman of mystery."

She turned her head away, staring through the windshield. "Why do you need me?"

Determined to lighten the mood, he said, "For one thing, you're not bad to look at."

"That's a terrible, unprofessional reason."

"I'd be lying if I told you that you aren't the prettiest partner I've ever had. I guess that's kind of a backhanded compliment."

"How so?"

"All my other partners have been guys who'd knock my teeth down my throat if I called them pretty."

She scoffed. "Typical guys."

"Bottom line, I enjoy being with you."

Her voice lightened. "I'm still waiting to hear a rational reason for why I should tag along with you."

"You aren't tagging along. You're a consultant, and you've already helped a lot. If you hadn't lured Channing to this meeting, I would have wasted time trying to get the kid to sit down for a talk. Your secret camera at the cabin provided an invaluable parameter for alibis. You're doing great. I'm the one who can't zero in on a profile."

"What about Channing?"

He was an unlikely suspect. His immaturity and indecisiveness might get him into a bar fight. But murder? Sloan doubted the kid would be capable of planning the complexities of Layla's murder. She'd been drugged and her body hidden before she was strangled, then the killer transported her to the cabin and arranged her in a pose. Not to mention the sophistication needed to set the bomb and the trigger.

At Monaco Street, Sloan turned right. Channing's girlfriend lived a couple of miles to the south. Even though they were engaged, she hadn't moved in with him. Sloan had to wonder if it was because Peter Channing idolized the "dolls." When he'd gazed at Brooke, his eyes were reverent. Every time he mentioned Franny, his voice oozed with emotion. He didn't want to kill these women. He wanted to worship them.

"On the surface, Channing is a typical kid. I don't see him committing murder, but he has a fixation on all of you, especially Franny."

"I know. It's weird, huh?"

"His engagement is a sign of recovery. There's another woman in his life, and he loves her. That should indicate he's ready to move on."

Sloan checked his rearview mirror and groaned.

"I don't believe this. That idiot Brancusi is tailing us."

She turned in her seat and peered through the back window. "I don't see him."

"In the left lane, two cars back. He's trying to be subtle." Sloan didn't want the filmmaker following them, mostly because Brancusi would think he'd influenced them by mentioning Channing's girlfriend. "Change of plans. We're going to FBI headquarters."

"Fine." She exhaled a sigh, an indication that she still wasn't one hundred percent on board with him.

"I wanted to go there, anyway. There's new evidence. It's about Zachary Doyle, the neighbor."

"The peeper," she said bitterly. "I hope you have him locked up."

"He's not able to travel." Though the peeper was a bad man, Sloan wouldn't wish this fate on anyone. "He has ALS. Most of the time, he's in a wheelchair, but he can move around enough to take care of himself and insists on staying alone at his cabin in the mountains. A home-care nurse comes by twice a week to help him with basic cleaning, cooking and supplies. He can't drive."

"Was he brought in to FBI headquarters?"

"We didn't think it was necessary. He's not a viable suspect because he's not physically capable of committing the crime. One of our agents went to his cabin and videotaped an interview with him."

He paused at a stoplight and studied her profile, trying to figure out how this information affected her. Signs of agitation were apparent. Her brow creased in a frown, and she chewed her lower lip. If viewing the video of Doyle would cause her to withdraw even more, he didn't want her to watch it.

"I hated him," she said quietly. "The man was a nightmare. He took a perverse pleasure in scaring me. But I'm sorry he's suffering."

"Is it worthwhile for you to watch the videotape?"

"I don't know," she said. "I never actually spoke to him. Apart from his leering at me through the window, I had no contact with him whatsoever."

At the next intersection, he made a U-turn and reversed his route—a move he hoped would help him evade Brancusi. "We need a new direction. Our initial premise was that the killer was someone who took part in the events from twelve years ago. Our suspects were Channing, Doyle and Brancusi."

"All of them have credible alibis."

"We have to break those alibis or find new suspects," he said.

"How do we do that?"

"Do you want a list?"

"Of course."

Her tidiness was adorably predictable. "First, I already mentioned needing info about Layla's current friends, professors and associates. Second, I want to take a look at other people who knew her twelve years ago."

"Number one is already done." She took her phone from her fanny pack and flipped through the screens. "I made a list of people she talked about and added some of her email contacts from her computer thumb drive."

"Any standouts?"

"She was close to a couple of her law professors and the other students in her study group. Their relationships were friendly. She and her last boyfriend broke up over a year ago. Layla had been completely focused on completing her degree. Nothing else was on the radar."

He'd expected as much. "Let's move on to my number two concern. What about other people from your past?"

"What about them?"

"I want to know about your memories, your subconscious thoughts. I want to climb inside your head and wander around."

"You might not like what you find, but okay. As long as it doesn't involve truth serum or hypnosis, I'll do it. For Layla."

If the videotape of the peeper didn't rattle her too much, Sloan had another plan for the day. He could spark Brooke's memories by going to the source, setting up a line of communication with the man who had destroyed her life—Martin Hardy.

INSIDE FBI HEADQUARTERS, Brooke felt safe but not comfortable. She didn't expect to be physically assaulted. However—as she well knew—there were other ways to be hurt. Prepared for trouble, her guard was up.

Sloan escorted her past the cubicles to a small office where SAC Keller sat behind the desk. He rose immediately, shook her hand and thanked her for helping in their investigation. The only personal touches in the room were a tall, large-leafed philodendron lurking in the corner and a photograph of Keller and a shiny blonde woman on the ski slopes. Keller's desktop was clean, with a minimum of supplies, a design choice that Brooke appreciated.

After they shook hands, she took a seat. "We don't seem to be having much luck with our suspects."

"Zachary Doyle turned out to be a dead end." Keller laced his fingers neatly on the desktop. "Doyle claimed that he lived alone when Hardy held you captive at the cabin. Is that true?"

"I don't know, but I didn't see anyone else."

"From time to time, Hardy brought other men with him to the cabin."

"Yes."

Her fingers twisted together on her lap, not reaching for the memory but not pushing it away. When Hardy showed up with his "friends," she wasn't allowed to look at them. She served the beer and whatever food they brought with them, and then she faded away.

The same was true for Layla and Sophia, who had been blindfolded and restrained while these strangers did unspeakable things. She dreaded the nights when she heard several car doors slam outside the cabin and Hardy burst through the door with his "friends." He showed an odd degree of loyalty to them, never giving their names to the court.

"At the time," Keller said, "you were unable to identify these men, not even to work with a sketch artist. Has your memory improved over the years? Do you recall any names or identifying marks? Maybe you saw a tattoo or a scar?"

"No."

"Concentrate, Brooke. Did any of them have an accent? Was there anything unusual about their voices?"

"If I had remembered," she said crisply, "I would have reported that information to Special Agent Gimbel."

Keeping his gaze fixed on her, he nodded slowly. Though he didn't aim the finger of guilt in her direction, she had the distinct impression that he didn't believe her, even though she'd done nothing to earn his distrust. She had no reason to hide information from the FBI. The opposite was true.

Determined not to speak first and break their silence, she locked eyes with him and straightened her shoulders, mimicking his erect posture. If he wanted a stare-down, she'd give it to him. Brooke was nothing if not patient. She could sit here for a solid five minutes without blinking.

Sloan interrupted, "Excuse me, sir. Is there new evidence about the other men who went to the cabin, maybe something on Layla's computer?"

"Only hints," he said, ending their showdown to look down at the pristine surface of his desk. "There's nothing substantial, but their existence opens many possibilities."

She shot a meaningful glance at Sloan. She'd also reviewed much of the data on Layla's thumb drives and found nothing to incriminate those faceless, nameless men.

"I agree about the possibilities," Sloan said. "Supposedly, these unknown subjects are out in the world, living their lives. How many were there, Brooke?"

"Over a period of seven months, Hardy must have brought friends home with him six or seven times." This was a fact she knew. Her therapist had talked with her about the stranger rapes a lot and found it hard to believe that Brooke hadn't been sexually assaulted. "I can't tell you how many men, because I don't know if they were different each time."

"I know what you're thinking," Sloan said to Keller, "and it's an elegant theory. Layla might have recognized one of these men and confronted him. That would make a strong motive for murder. She could accuse him of rape."

"Would her murder fit the profile for one of those men?"

"Not a good fit," Sloan said. "When her murderer attacked, she wasn't sexually assaulted or brutalized, which is what I'd expect from a rapist. Postmortem, Layla's body was posed and handled with extreme care."

Keller cleared his throat. "Profiling isn't an exact science."

"Which is why we'll look into your theory, and I'll talk to the other women," Sloan said. "In the meantime, I'd like to show Brooke the video of Zachary Doyle so she can verify his statements."

"If his statement triggers any memories…"

"You'll be the first to know," she said as she rose from the chair. "Technically, you'll be the second, because Sloan will be with me, and I'll tell him first."

She gave him a friendly grin, hoping to call a truce between them. But SAC Keller didn't crack a smile. He issued an order. "Sloan, have one of the techs set up the video. And I'll want a full report on Peter Channing before the end of the day."

"You got it."

As he hustled her down the corridor, she asked, "What a pill! How can you stand to work with him?"

"We're not pals, but Keller isn't a bad guy. He's ambitious and wants results. When he doesn't get answers, he tends to be cranky."

To say the least. She followed him through the maze of hallways and staircases to a small room with a table, a credenza, a couple of chairs and a thirty-six-inch video screen hanging on the wall. Sloan left for a few moments, which gave her time to take a deep breath and consider whether or not she was doing the smart thing by watching the video of Doyle.

Dr. Joan would say no. Seeing Doyle would reopen a lot of old wounds. Delving deeper into the past was a terrifying prospect. For twelve years she'd tried her hardest to forget. But if staring into the face of the peeper would help solve the crime, she had to do it.

Sloan returned with a friendly tech guy who loaded the video, handed a remote to Sloan and asked him to return it when they were done. The tech guy closed the door.

Taking a seat beside her at a small table, Sloan aimed the remote at the screen. "I can turn off the video any time you want, just let me know."

"I can take it." At least, she thought she could.

A silent image appeared frozen on the screen.

Though he wasn't seen below the waist, she could tell that Zachary Doyle was sitting in a wheelchair. He was still ugly, and the disease had taken a toll. He was gaunt to the point of emaciation. Deep furrows scored his brow and circled his mouth. His lips pulled back from his yellowed teeth.

She leaned way back in her chair, wanting to be as far away from the image on the screen as possible. Twelve years ago, he terrified her in the night. On purpose, he chose to behave like a monster. The horrific consequences of his disease weren't his fault, but she couldn't help thinking that his outer deterioration reflected the evil inside him.

When Sloan placed a steadying hand on her arm, she flinched.

"Should I start the video?" he asked.

She nodded. "Go ahead."

"Are you sure? You don't have to watch this."

"For Layla's sake, I do."

The vivid image on the screen moved slowly and with great effort. His entire body shook with a violent cough that made it sound like death was near, but when he started talking, he sounded stronger. Who knew that he had a nice voice?

Doyle repeated the interviewer's question, "What's that? Did you want to know who watched those little monkeys when Hardy went out? It wasn't me. I can tell you that. We weren't close neighbors, no, sir, not me. I can't even see his cabin from my place."

"Did you consider him a friend?" the interviewer asked.

"I kept to myself, and he did the same. A couple of times he asked me to watch over his cabin while he went into town, but I never went inside. Even if I'd wanted to, I couldn't. All the doors were locked up tight. The windows, too. Nobody could get in."

She whispered, "And nobody could get out."

When the media rolled out their story, people asked why it took so long for them to break away from the cabin. After all, there were six of them and only one of him. Couldn't they have overpowered him?

Those people didn't know what it was like. The physical restraints and locks were only part of their captivity. They were trapped by terror— a bone-deep fear of punishment and Hardy's cruel threats. She was still held back by the terror of her memories. Until she could forget, she was in a cage.

Chapter Fifteen

Brooke suppressed the urge to flee from the room. Gripping the arms of her chair, she forced herself to watch the videotape of Zachary Doyle, who talked about how Hardy was almost always at the cabin, never gone for more than a day or two.

The interviewer asked, "Did you ever see the girls?"

His rheumy eyes glanced away as though to evade that question. Brooke knew what he'd done. His face appeared in her window late at night, and he'd laughed at her. But that wasn't what he told the FBI interviewer.

"Can't recall," he said. "Maybe I caught a glimpse now and again."

Brooke was pleased when the interviewer didn't let him off the hook. "Did you ever look in the windows?"

"Like a peeping Tom?" His bony hand wiped spittle from the corner of his mouth. "I'm a God-fearing man. I'd never do such a thing."

"Yes, you did," she shouted at the screen.

"Again and again and again, you stared in the window. You did it."

The interviewer continued, "One of the women reported seeing your face."

"I'm not surprised that she'd lie. Those girls were real messed up." He poked his ugly face closer to the camera. "I'm a good person."

A blinding rage exploded in her head. How could this monster claim to be decent? Whether or not he denied it, Doyle had known what Hardy was doing to them. Doyle had seen the shackles and chains. He could have rescued them at any time.

"I've got references, plenty of people think highly of me," he said. "I used to sing in the choir at church, and the reverend will stand up for me. Hey, that reminds me. One of the church ladies brought an armload of girls' clothes to Hardy's cabin. Another time, she left some food on the porch."

"Do you remember her name?"

"Don't know."

Brooke reined in her anger. "He's not lying about the woman."

"Did you ever see the church lady?" Sloan asked.

"No, but I remember the cast-off clothing and a huge pan of lasagna. We rationed the slices, ate it for days."

They watched the interview for another fifteen minutes until Doyle suffered a severe coughing attack, and it was over. When the screen went dark, she hoped she would never see his face again.

Sloan lightly stroked her shoulder. "Are you all right?"

"I wish we'd gotten more from the interview. He never mentioned the other men."

"But he talked about his good buddy the reverend. And a woman from the church. We'll check them out."

She gazed up at him. "I don't even know where the church is. This is so frustrating. What kind of evidence can we get from a church lady who was blind enough to drop off lasagna and not come inside?"

"She might have noticed something."

"It was twelve years ago. How will you track her down?"

"That's the job." The warmth of his smile lifted her spirits. When he leaned close, she could smell the clean scent of sandalwood soap. He whispered in her ear, "Try to believe what I'm telling you. We usually nab the bad guy."

"I hope so."

She needed justice to be done.

SLOAN CHECKED THE address for Channing's girlfriend again before driving away from FBI headquarters. He slipped the SUV into gear and headed toward the exit. In his opinion, the "unknown subject" theory favored by Keller didn't have much traction. He suspected that if Layla had recognized one of her abusers, she would have told Brooke or one of the other women. That seemed to be the pattern. When talking to him, Franny had described how she saw Peter Channing in the grocery store. But she'd given a similar version of that story to Brooke a long time ago.

These women were close. They watched out for each other and didn't keep secrets. The only real conflict he'd seen was between the twins, who didn't really dislike each other. They were born to be best friends. If there was a threat to one, the others would know about it, with the possible exception of Sophia, because she lived in Las Vegas. He made a mental note to put through another call to her.

And he'd talk to the others. He'd already contacted Gimbel and asked him to help pry open any hidden memories the women might have about the men who occasionally came home with Hardy.

Leaving headquarters, he drove from the underground parking lot, passed the gatehouse, where he waved to the armed men inside, and merged into traffic. It was another beautiful, sunny day, filled with light and a view of the distant mountains. After turning on the air-conditioning, he glanced over at Brooke. The fury she'd displayed when watching Doyle had passed. She seemed relaxed.

"What does the FBI know about Channing's fiancée?" she asked.

"Her name is Karen Galloway," he said. "She goes by Kiki."

"How long have they been dating?"

"I don't have many details. Ms. Galloway was interviewed by a cop who did us a favor by stopping at her house and having her verify Channing's alibi. All I have are the basics from her driver's license. She's blonde with hazel eyes and older than him, pushing forty."

"I've got to wonder what she sees in the kid. Channing is so immature."

"I've heard that women like the boyish type."

"Not me. Little boys are unpredictable and boring at the same time. I know that doesn't sound possible, but it is. I've seen a little boy try to stick an unpeeled banana up his nose. Totally unpredictable. Who would think of such a thing? Then he peeled it and tried again. After that, the boy spent ten minutes telling me what he'd just done. Boring, very boring."

He was glad to hear her talking about something other than murder. He wanted to build a relationship that went beyond their shared interest in the investigation. "What do you like in a man?"

"He needs to be an adult who is responsible and smart, capable of holding up his end of an intelligent conversation. Also, a gentleman."

"You like a guy who holds the door for you?"

"Sure." She flashed a grin. "You almost always open my car door."

He'd take that as a compliment. "What about physically?"

"Agent Sloan, are you asking what turns me on?"

He braked for a stoplight, cocked his head in her direction and studied her beautiful face. Her eyes weren't visible because she'd put on a pair of sunglasses from her fanny pack, but her smile encouraged him to tease. "Do you prefer tall men who wear suits?"

"Definitely tall," she said, "but not big and muscle-bound. And I'm fond of a well-fitted suit—better yet, a tuxedo."

"I don't have a tux, but I own a US Navy dress white uniform."

"A man in uniform, very nice." She lowered her glasses and looked over the rims. Her fluttering eyelashes were meant as a joke but were sexy all the same. "And what do you like in a woman?"

"I could say black hair and blue eyes. Under the current circumstances, that doesn't exactly narrow the field, so I'll be more specific." He paused, aware that he was crossing boundaries. The safe move would be to back off, but he wanted to be honest with her. "You have everything I look for in a woman."

She flipped her sunglasses over her eyes and stared through the windshield. Quietly, she said something he couldn't quite make out.

It could have been "you're bad" or "I'm sad."

He wanted to believe she said "I'm glad" but decided not to push for an explanation. They were too close to Kiki Galloway's house to engage in a complicated conversation. "We're almost there."

The older neighborhood was typical of those built during Denver's post-WWII housing boom. A row of two-bedroom brick houses was set back from the street. The lawns had begun to yellow due to watering restrictions. Ms. Galloway's bungalow was midway down the block.

When he parked at the curb, Brooke made a tsk-tsk noise. "This could be a nice place, but it's been neglected. The gutters are falling off, the paint on the trim is chipped and the sidewalk is cracked. I'm surprised she hasn't recruited Channing to make repairs."

"Could be she's waiting until after they're married." When Brooke put her hand on the door handle, he reached across her. "Don't open it. That's my job."

"Being a gentleman?"

"And a bodyguard."

He jumped out of the SUV and circled to her side. After he opened her car door, he escorted her up the sidewalk to meet Kiki Galloway.

STANDING AT THE screen door, Brooke noticed that Kiki wasn't much of a gardener, and she didn't put away her tools. Her car—in need of a wash—was parked in the driveway outside the garage, not unusual for a Saturday. Brooke wondered what she did for a living. Was she expecting her young fiancé to step up and support her?

When Kiki opened the door, Brooke was dumbfounded. Instead of meeting a hazel-eyed blonde, Brooke shook hands with a woman whose black hair and blue eyes matched her own. "You must be Peter Channing's fiancée."

"And you're Brooke Josephson. Please come in."

Unable to take her eyes off the woman who looked younger than the age on her driver's license, Brooke barely noticed the furnishings. There was no central air-conditioning and two fans whirred ineffectively, which was probably why Kiki was dressed in scanty shorts and a tube top. She was an attractive lady in good physical condition with muscular arms and legs. Why had she dyed her hair and put on blue contact lenses?

They sat at a dining room table that was cluttered but nowhere near as messy as the table at Franny's place. Sloan took his spiral notebook from his jacket pocket and started asking her questions about Channing's actions since Tuesday. Other than his job at Taco Guac, he seemed to have spent all his time with Kiki.

She pointed to a big, empty cardboard box in the middle of the living room and said, "We went shopping on Wednesday and bought a nightstand that needed to be put together. It was hot, sweaty work, and I rewarded my man with a big glass of fresh lemonade."

"Two lemons and a cup of sugar," Brooke said.

"That's right," Kiki said. "How did you know?"

She'd followed that simple recipe frequently when they were in the cabin. "I used to make it that way. Channing liked it."

"You were the little mama." She rolled her fake blue eyes. "My sweetie said you were bossy."

Seven months of captivity hadn't been a game of playing house. She'd never wanted to be in charge and take care of them. Any person with a drop of sensitivity would understand that she did whatever necessary to survive. By calling her bossy, Kiki was trying to provoke her.

Sloan moved on to his questions about the next day. "On Friday, you told the police that you and Channing were together in the morning. He went to work from nine until two. Is that correct?"

"That's what I told them. I felt bad for Peter. His taco truck gets so hot." She tossed her shoulder-length black hair. "Are you hot, Agent Sloan? You can take off your jacket."

"Where were you from nine until two?"

"I can't remember."

"Oh, come on," Brooke said. "It was only yesterday."

"You should know. That's when your friend got herself killed, right?"

Anger surged through her, but Brooke held herself in check. This woman's crazy, deep connection to Channing cast doubt on his alibi. And there was another possibility—they could have been working together.

While Channing was at work, Kiki could have made the drive to the cabin. She had the muscles that would have been needed to carry Layla, who was thin. When it came right down to it, Kiki could have done the murder all by herself.

"What do you do for a living?" Brooke hoped she had a job with access to bomb-making materials, maybe in an electronics store.

"I used to be a checkout clerk at the supermarket, but I've been out of work for a couple of months. It's just as well. Planning a wedding takes a lot of time."

"Why did Channing make you dye your hair?"

"He didn't." She rolled her eyes, again. "He's my fiancé, not my boss."

"You did it yourself? To look like us?"

"You make it sound so weird."

Because it was. "Can you explain?"

"Peter always talked about you girls like you were his sisters. He especially liked little Franny. And I thought it would be funny to dress up like a little girl and do my hair. I liked the way it turned out, and then I added the contacts. When Peter saw me, he was over the moon. Best sex ever."

"You had to know the illusion wouldn't last,"

Brooke said. "You could never truly replace Franny in his affections."

"He tried to get ahold of you gals for years. He told me that after the trial you disappeared, and nobody would help him find you. When he asked for an address, the FBI threatened him. He was only twelve years old and being pushed around by the feds. No wonder he took off when he heard they wanted to contact him. So sorry, Agent Sloan, but Peter's experiences with the FBI have been all bad."

He acknowledged her words with a quick nod but didn't bother to apologize or defend the actions of other agents. "He was corresponding with Layla via email."

"He wasn't looking for her but stumbled across her address when he was looking for a cheapo lawyer."

"Why? Was he having legal problems?"

"I told him we should sue my landlord because Peter tripped on a broken piece of the sidewalk and sprained his ankle. But he forgot all about the lawyer when he found Layla's name. He was so happy when he sent that first email."

"And she never responded," Brooke said. "That must have upset him."

"He'd never get mad at any of you. His perfect little dolls, the Hardy Dolls." This time she didn't bother to cover her hostility with the cutesy eye roll. "You think you're so special, but you're not."

"You must have hated Layla."

"I never met her," Kiki said.

"Were you jealous?"

"Ha! My sweetie is completely devoted to me. I'm his whole world. You girls are just figments from the past."

Sloan rose from his chair at the table. "I'll only ask one more time, Kiki. Where were you on Friday after Channing left?"

"Seriously, do I need an alibi?"

"It wouldn't hurt."

"No big deal. I did a couple of errands and went to the gym. Talk to my personal trainer."

"His name?"

"Is this really necessary? He probably won't be around. You can talk to somebody at the front desk."

"Give me his name or you're under arrest."

She muttered, "Shane Waters."

Brooke knew that Sloan would verify that alibi. He must be having the same suspicions about this phony Hardy Doll. She was jealous and nasty enough that Brooke felt a glimmer of sympathy for Channing. The feeling passed quickly. He could have been working with Kiki to hurt Layla and take his revenge for years of being ignored.

Chapter Sixteen

When they returned to the SUV, Brooke blurted, "What a horrible woman! She's got to be a suspect, right?"

"Oh, yeah." Sloan slipped the car into gear and mentally mapped out the route to her house, which was about five miles away—ironically close, considering Channing's supposedly desperate search for the women he considered sisters. "I'll arrange with Keller to have Kiki's alibi verified. A visit to the gym is hard to prove. She might have checked in and then left."

"To dispose of the body. Oh, no, how could I say that? The body?" Her hands flew up and covered her face. "Layla was so much more than a murder victim, more than a collection of tissue, organs and blood. She was my best friend."

He reached across the console to rub her shoulder. She'd been going through hell. Not only was she mourning her friend, but Brooke had been hammered by experiences that reopened the past and retraumatized her. He didn't know how much more she could take before she shattered.

Earlier today, he'd considered putting her in touch with Martin Hardy via live video feed from the prison, but that might be a step too far. She hadn't seen him for twelve years, but that might not be long enough. Was there a set amount of time to pass before she could face the devil who had tormented her and scarred her for life?

Sloan knew that if he asked, she'd agree to the interview with Hardy, no matter how much it might hurt. Her overriding concern was to find Layla's killer. That was her mantra. She'd told him a half dozen times that she'd do anything for Layla. *Anything!* Always putting the needs of others ahead of her own, she wasn't great at protecting herself. He wanted to keep her safe, but this wasn't his decision.

She stiffened her spine and hid her expressive eyes behind her sunglasses. "I'm okay."

You're not fooling me. "If you say so."

"So, Mr. Profiler, does Kiki fit the bill?"

"As you mentioned, she's a horrible human being. Nice guns, though."

"Are you talking about her muscular arms? I can't believe you focused on that."

"Her physical assets were hard to miss. She put it all on display." He was a man. Of course, he noticed. "Oddly enough, I don't think her purpose was seduction. All that posing was meant to intimidate."

"Did it work?"

He shrugged. "I could take her."

Though he hadn't altogether been joking, he appreciated Brooke's chuckle. Her mood was returning to something less intense. "Let's get back to Kiki's profile," she said. "Could she be the murderer?"

"You can't put much stock in a quickie analysis, but here goes." He cleared his throat. "Kiki Galloway is a master manipulator, very competitive and demanding. These traits make her the perfect mate for an immature guy like Channing. He needs to be told what to do, and she's happy to give the orders."

"That makes logical sense," she said. "But I don't believe he'd obey a command to murder a woman he cared about."

"Very true, and murder wouldn't be her first choice when it came to besting an opponent. She'd prefer a competition for her man's affection. She might even arrange a meeting between Layla and Channing."

"And then what?"

"I have no basis for further speculation," he said. "Everything I'm saying is pure fiction and can't be acted upon legally."

"I still want to hear it."

While they were sitting at Kiki's messy table,

he had envisioned a possible scenario. "Suppose Channing arranges to meet Layla or he ambushes her. She freaks out and he drugs her. That's when Kiki steps in. Using information stolen from Layla, she makes the threatening phone calls to Franny and does the weird stalking stuff."

"And the honking car in my garage," she reminded.

"A woman like Kiki would enjoy the chance to terrorize all of you. At some point, she'd realize that she couldn't let Layla go free to identify her. Then, Kiki might strangle Layla, cover the ligature mark and tell Channing that she didn't know how Layla died. All the unusual moving of Layla from place to place and finally taking her to the cabin would fit with Kiki's manipulative patterns. The weird machinations make me suspect her."

"Like you said, there's no proof. It's just a hunch, but better than nothing."

As they came nearer to her house, he shifted to a different topic. "This afternoon, I'll spend some time at your house, talking to the others. But I need to return to headquarters."

"To arrange for surveillance on Kiki?"

"And to file my reports. Then I need to dig through some fairly tedious police work, reviewing potential suspects."

"How do you decide who's a suspect?"

"Keller has been coordinating interviews with

professors, neighbors and associates who had a connection with Layla. If any of them have criminal records or other suspicious leanings, I'll go deeper, see if they fit a profile and maybe pay them a visit."

"Like we did with Kiki," she said. "What else?"

"After a comprehensive computer search, I'll review every person who visited or corresponded with Martin Hardy during the last twelve years. Beyond that, I'll study possible copycat crimes and unsolved murders that fit the profile for this investigation."

"Why would anyone want to copy a scum bucket like Hardy?"

Her innocence touched him. In spite of everything she'd been through, Brooke still had a hard time imaging the sick and twisted motives that drove some people. The world was populated by monsters: sadists, pedophiles, predators and abusers. A confrontation with Hardy via video feed would be traumatic for her. He should forget about it, concentrate instead on keeping her safe. But he felt there might be something to be gained from talking to Hardy. "Do you ever think of him?"

"Every day." A muscle in her jaw twitched. "Sometimes, I think I see him in the distance or hear his voice, even when I'm alone at night."

"Last night?"

"I fell into bed and slept like a log, and that's

unusual for me. I often lie awake with a myriad of details rushing across my brain. I think I was too overwhelmed to dream. Yesterday I learned that my best friend was dead, went to the murder scene and nearly got blown up." Her head cocked to one side as she turned toward him. "I'm guessing that you see terrible things on a daily basis. Does it ever get to you?"

Sometimes he wished he could pull the covers over his head and not get out of bed, but he knew firsthand that he couldn't hide from injustice. "It's my job."

When he heard the *thwap-thwap* of helicopter blades, he looked up at a news chopper that should have been reporting traffic jams on the highway. Instead, the helo hovered over Brooke's house. What the hell did they expect to see? On her street, the media trucks and reporters formed a perimeter around her property.

A barricade blocked the end of the street. Sloan showed his shield to a cop, who cleared the way after a brief exchange on his walkie-talkie. As they drove through the crowd, Brooke scrunched down in the passenger seat and held up her hand to shield her face from the cameras.

"You've done this before," he said.

"Sadly, yes."

No wonder she'd chosen an occupation that allowed her to work from home. This kind of scrutiny would make anybody want to lock the doors and throw away the keys. Though he drove into the driveway and parked as close to the house as possible, there was a ten-yard distance between his SUV and the front door.

"Give me your jacket," she said. "I'm going to put it over my head so they can't get a clear photo."

When they left the car, he heard the media people calling her name, trying to get her to turn around. He walked in front of her, shielding her from their view. With every step, he was more and more grateful to be anonymous.

Inside the house, they joined Franny, Lancaster and Gimbel, who were sitting at the dining room table. Franny left her seat, dashed toward them and threw her arms around Brooke.

"Are you okay?" she asked. "Where have you been?"

Brooke cast him a sidelong glance. "Can I tell her everything?"

"I don't see why not."

She faced her perky friend and said, "I talked to Peter Channing."

"Omigod, omigod, omigod." She ran to the front staircase and shouted up, "Moira and Megan, get down here. Brooke has news."

Sloan needed to get back to headquarters. He pulled Gimbel aside and asked him to talk to each of the women about their memories of the unknown men that Hardy had brought to the cabin.

"Twelve years ago," Gimbel said, "I asked a million questions about those guys and got nothing that would identify them. But it doesn't hurt to ask again. Memories change."

"If they come up with anything significant—"

"I'll give you a full report," the retired agent said. "This isn't my first rodeo."

His comment was fitting. In his jeans, boots and battered hat, he looked like an old cowhand. "I appreciate your help."

"I'd do anything for these ladies."

"So would I," Lancaster said, unapologetic about eavesdropping and intruding on a private conversation. "Is there anything I can do?"

In spite of the offer to be useful, Sloan didn't like or trust this guy. "Why are you here?"

"I thought I could be their spokesperson with the reporters. I just want to help."

To help his career. With the bevy of media in attendance, Lancaster was dying to step up to the microphones and make sure everybody saw his shiny bald head on the evening news. More than likely, he'd been waiting for Brooke to come home and give the okay. "If you make a statement, you need to state clearly that your pronouncements are not sanctioned by the FBI."

Before Sloan left, he spoke to Brooke and promised he would return later tonight. If she thought of anything, she should call him. He wanted to pose the question about doing the video feed conversation with Hardy, but he still wasn't sure what to say.

It was a big risk, and he didn't want to hurt her.

HOURS LATER, BROOKE sat behind her desk in her office. She had considered going through files on the thumb drives to look at photos but decided she couldn't bear the images of Layla smiling and laughing. The sorrow was too raw, too new. She didn't want to face the pain.

Instead, she watched the clock and waited for Sloan to return. He'd called, said he'd be over at about nine o'clock—which was in seven minutes—and he'd asked if that was too late. She was okay with having him show up at nine, ten or midnight. Last night she'd been exhausted, but not tonight. Tonight, she was wired.

Today had been productive. They'd eliminated Zachary Doyle as a suspect. Peter Channing seemed to be in the clear until they met his fiancée and started considering them as a team. Since Brancusi's alibi had already cleared, the only suspects connected with the past were the sick, depraved, nameless men who had come to the cabin with Hardy.

Evidence was leading Sloan in different directions. He had to consider Layla's friends and colleagues as well as people who might have visited Hardy in prison and the vast general population of copycats who wanted to emulate Hardy's cruelty. The further afield the investigation went, the less Sloan would be able to use her assistance.

Brooke knew their time together was limited, but she wasn't ready to say goodbye. Their kiss this morning had opened a window of possibility that she hadn't considered for years. Not only was she attracted to the tall, lean federal agent with the intriguing gray-silver-green eyes, but he also aroused her. The unsatisfying sexual experiences she'd had in the past might no longer define her as a woman. Sloan might be the key.

Her memory skipped to thoughts of another key—the one Channing had given her. When she closed her eyes, she imagined the feel of the cold metal in the palm of her hand. She could have used that key to escape, but she'd been too scared to take a chance.

So much of her life had been spent being safe, taking precautions and avoiding danger. It might be time to take a chance. Tonight, she'd arrange for privacy for her and Sloan. And she would make the advances on him. Was that manipulative? Was she turning into Kiki?

There was a knock on the door. Lancaster poked his head inside and asked, "Are you working on anything?"

"No." She hadn't even turned on her computer.

"I'm getting ready to leave. Is there anything you want me to tell the reporters?"

"There's nothing to say."

"Decisions have been made," he pointed out. "Moira, Megan and her daughter will be leaving tomorrow and staying at Megan's house."

"I don't think it's a good idea to say where we are or where we might be going."

"If Gimbel had allowed me to listen while he was talking to all of you, I'd have better information to pass along. When he was leaving, I asked him if there was anything new, and he brushed me off. The big news is that you talked to Peter Channing."

"Any information about suspects should come from the FBI." From what Sloan had told her, SAC Keller enjoyed seeing his face on the news almost as much as her lawyer. "Please respect our privacy."

"You have bodyguards. You'll be fine."

Safety was a virtue. She'd believed in that rule for most of her life. She gave him a nod and glanced toward her blank computer screen. "I'll have to say good-night."

"Don't worry. I'll be back tomorrow."

She didn't really want to see him again, but his expertise was useful. The clock on her wall said four minutes past nine. Had Sloan changed his mind about coming here? Maybe he'd found a promising lead and needed to follow up. That would be good news, of course—she wanted the killer caught. But she didn't want her time with Sloan to end.

Leaving the office, she went into the entry-way, where one of the bodyguards had stationed himself. He sat on a lower step of the staircase. When he saw her, he held up the computer tab-let with the camera surveillance so she could see the view of the front door. With a grin, he said, "Looks like you have a visitor."

In enhanced night vision, she watched the screen as Sloan crossed from his SUV to her porch. His loosened necktie was the only sign of disarray after this long, stressful day. An un-familiar but pleasant sensation fluttered inside her rib cage.

Her heart jumped. Filled with hope, she for-got all else.

Chapter Seventeen

Brooke wasn't exactly sure how she and Sloan had gotten from the entryway to the basement. Floating on air wasn't literally possible, but she lacked awareness of movement and physical sensation. She couldn't feel her bare feet touching the floor or her muscles flexing as she walked. Her vision blurred. Though inhaling and exhaling, she wasn't aware of breathing and hadn't heard her voice as she welcomed him into her home and suggested they go somewhere private to talk.

Inside the panic room, she closed and locked the door. They were alone.

In her mind, she'd built up this moment when they would be together to such an extent that her brain fogged. *What came next?* She should say something brilliant, reveal a hidden talent or twirl like a fidget spinner. But she was frozen. When he pulled down the wall bed and reclined upon it, she couldn't think of one single reason why she should be hyperventilating. And yet, she was gasping.

"Are you okay?" he asked.

"Uh-huh." On stiff legs, she crossed the tiny room and plunked down beside him.

"Gimbel gave me his preliminary report over the phone. He didn't learn anything new."

"Uh-huh." She couldn't think. *What's wrong with my brain?* Was this what happened to people who got sexually aroused? Did they turn into drooling morons?

"Franny and the twins told him they never saw the men Hardy brought by. He locked the younger girls up in their room."

"That's right." She dug her fingernails into the palm of her hand, thinking that the resulting pain would wake her up.

"Gimbel really likes all of you, and he's deeply concerned about your safety, both physical and psychological. Layla's murder and the threats are traumatic. You know that."

"Uh-huh." She had to stop mumbling. *Snap out of it!* The time had come to untangle her tongue and start making sense. "When things settle down, we'll make appointments with our therapists. I need grounding. Believe me, Sloan, that's an understatement. And I'll make sure the others are okay."

"I'm worried, too," he said. "I don't want to do anything to make this harder for you."

"Great!" Inhaling a breath, she tried her best to find her center and pull herself together. Her psychological issues were *not* what she wanted to talk about with Sloan. Diverting his focus away from her glaring problems, she asked, "What about your afternoon? Did you learn anything new at headquarters?"

"There's stuff I should follow up on. I should schedule personal interviews with people from your list of Layla's associates. As for the database of possible copycats, I never really bought into that profile, not for this case. Martin Hardy never killed anybody. If somebody really wanted to copy him, they'd be staging abductions."

"Speaking of the devil," she said, referring to Hardy, "did you discover any suspicious people who visited the prison?"

"A few, and there were people who wrote him letters." A frown tugged at the corners of his mouth. "There's something we need to talk about. It concerns Hardy."

On a scale of one to ten, a discussion about Hardy was ten times ten in the negative. Not something she wanted to chat about. "Right now, I just want to relax. You know, Sloan, it's just you and me in this room. It's okay for you to take off your necktie."

"Yeah?" He cocked an eyebrow.

"Please."

"It's funny. I never thought I'd grow up to be a guy who wore a suit every day." After he removed his holster and gun, he took off his jacket and neatly draped it on a chair beside the bed. He tugged the knot on his tie, unfastened the patterned fabric from his neck and rolled it into a ball that he tucked into his jacket pocket.

Watching him undress in such a tidy manner excited her so much that her throat constricted. Her voice was as a whisper, which she hoped sounded sexy. "Better?"

"A little." He loosened his collar button and a few more, enough to give her a glimpse of his dark, curly chest hair. A moment of quiet enveloped them. There was nothing more to say. Action was required.

He scanned the supplies that packed her panic room. "You did a good job in here. It looks like you've got all the basics covered."

"And some of the luxuries."

She reached into a woven picnic hamper beside the bed and took out a bottle of merlot, which she handed to him along with a corkscrew. Her hands were trembling too much to open the bottle. This move was brazen, forward and not like her at all. She couldn't believe she'd thought ahead and brought the wine down here.

While he applied the corkscrew, she produced two crystal wineglasses from the basket. They came from an expensive set that she seldom had a chance to use. After tapping them lightly together to hear the ping, she met his gaze. "Too obvious?"

"Your intentions are clear." He pulled the cork.

"And I'll be equally transparent. I want to share this wine with you. I want to kiss you again. Frankly, I want more than a kiss. But it's not possible."

"That's too bad." Her soaring spirits took a nosedive. "I don't put on this kind of show for just anybody."

"I'm a federal officer, and you're part of the case that I'm investigating. It's wrong for me to use my position to start a relationship."

She knew the rules and limitations but had hoped they could ignore them. For once in her life, she wanted to color outside the lines, but she understood the restrictions. In a small voice, she asked, "If we'd met under different circumstances, would you be interested in me?"

"Hell, yes. I'd send you a dozen red roses and a pound of chocolate truffles. If things were different, I'd hire a carriage and take you to a five-star hotel, where we'd order oysters and strawberries from room service and make love all night." He poured the shimmering red wine. "Cheers."

They clinked glasses and sipped. Though she wasn't much of a drinker, she liked the crisp, fruity flavor. She drank more deeply as she considered the seductive fantasy that had rolled off his tongue so easily. "Have you ever done that before? Taken a carriage ride and feasted on room service?"

"Never." His lips curved in a grin that was sexier than it ought to be. "You inspire me."

She hadn't intended to be an ethereal muse. Her plan had been to get down and dirty. Holding her wineglass up to the light, she swirled the ruby liquid. "This comes from a winery on the western slope."

"I like it."

She drained her glass and held it out to be refilled. "I have a serious question for you, Agent Sloan."

"Shoot."

"You're good at profiling everybody else. What about yourself?"

"Self-analysis is a part of psychology training. I've heard it said that the reason people go into this field is to deal with their own mental and emotional issues."

"Let me guess," she said. "You're obsessive-compulsive, like me."

"I like to think I'm efficient and neat."

"So do I." She took another glug of wine, aware that she was drinking too fast. "And you're super empathetic. It's like you have your own personal traumatic stress to deal with."

"Right again," he said, too quickly.

"What happened to you, Sloan?"

He peered into his crystal glass as though looking for answers. "We'll talk about it another time."

Avoiding an uncomfortable situation was a tactic she knew well. She understood the wall he put up and his unwillingness to talk about how his life had been forever changed by a terrible experience. Like her, he was still struggling with the aftermath. She stepped away from the topic. There was no point in banging her head against an unbreakable wall of defense.

She contented herself with conversation. Mostly, they talked about food. Though he was relatively new in Denver, he'd been to more restaurants than she had. He confided that he wanted to learn how to ski this winter, and she offered to join him. All the while, they continued drinking the wine.

"Do you know what I want?" She gave him a loose-lipped smile. "I want to stop calling you Agent Sloan. It's too formal, and we're friends."

"Friends? Yes." He tapped the last drop of wine from the bottle.

"Justin?"

"What is it, Brooke?"

Saying his name felt so familiar, as though she knew a secret. Justin Sloan reclined against the pillows on her pull-down bed with his collar buttons unfastened and a wineglass in his hand, looking like an advertisement for pheromone-based cologne. "You know how the firemen have those sexy calendars? Does the FBI have an Agent of the Month?"

"It's not really our thing."

"It should be. I'd buy a hundred copies and use them for wallpaper."

She tilted sideways and set her empty glass on the floor. She'd need both hands free for what she had planned. Though he'd told her, in straightforward terms, that nothing was going to happen, she figured she might as well try to change his mind. Looking down, she unfastened the buttons on her pale blue blouse. Underneath, she wore a black lace bra. With her blouse open, she pushed the fabric aside to give him a clear view.

"Beautiful," he said.

She was pleased to note that his voice sounded as strangled as hers had been when she first came into the panic room. She should have elegantly and silently accepted the compliment, but the wine made her chatty. "About a year ago, I got this bra when I set out to seduce the man I'd been dating. The seduction didn't end well. The guy turned out to be a dud."

"He didn't deserve you."

"Thank you, Justin. That was precisely the right thing to say."

He set down his own wineglass and moved closer to her on the bed. With the back of his hand, he stroked the line of her jaw and throat. His hand glided lower. Gently, he caressed the swell of her breasts above her lace bra.

His touch ignited a million sensations, from the tingling across her skin to the hard throbbing of her heart. Excitement spiraled inside her. This excitement was the start of what she wanted, and she was greedy for more. When she touched him, she didn't use as much finesse. As quickly as possible, she unbuttoned his shirt and yanked it off. She savored the sight of his bared chest.

"When I first met you," she said, "I never thought we'd end up like this."

"I don't believe that. Within five minutes of saying hello, you had my shirt off."

"Not intentionally."

When he slipped her blouse off her shoulders, he held her upper arms so she couldn't move away while he kissed the line of her collarbone. Slowly, he eased her down on the bed beneath him. The subtle pressure of his mouth created a wave of pleasure that surged and ebbed through her body. She arched her back. Her breasts thrust closer to his chest, and she felt her nipples tighten into hard nubs.

She tried to break away from him, not because she wanted to escape but so she could tear off her bra and press her naked flesh against him. He restrained her. The moment of struggle against his superior strength was even more pleasurable when he released his hold and she flung her arms around him, pulling him down on top of her.

Her mouth joined with his for a burning kiss. For the first time in her life, she knew what real passion felt like. She spread her thighs, needing to be closer to him. And he wanted her, too. When his erection rubbed against her, she reached down and stroked his hard shaft.

He made a sound deep in his throat that was midway between a growl and a sigh. And then he pushed himself upright, putting distance between them. Breathing hard, he sat on the edge of the bed. "This isn't right, Brooke."

She lay back on the pillows, humiliated. What had she been thinking? She crossed her arms over her chest to hide her fancy lace bra. She wished she could blame her behavior on the wine, but that wasn't exactly true. Her inhibitions were lowered, but she hadn't gone unconscious. Brooke had known what she was doing.

She rolled onto her side with her back to him. "Agent Sloan, would you please leave."

The bed creaked when he stood. Though she wasn't watching, she knew he was walking toward the door. The last time they were in this room, she'd explained how to open the lock. Like many of her secrets, she'd willingly shared that with him.

Her attempted seduction was a mistake, foolish. All that was left was to pick up the shreds of her pride and try to weave them into whole cloth. She sat on the bed and put on her blouse. "Why are you still here?"

"There's something I need to tell you," he said.

"Not many people know about this, and I'd appreciate if you'd keep the information to yourself."

"Sure thing." She infused her tone with sarcasm. "It must be awful to have everyone know the most private details of your life. But wait, I know exactly what that's like."

"Look at me, Brooke."

With the final button on her shirt fastened, she turned her gaze toward the tall man standing beside the door to the panic room. She wanted to be angry at him, but it was impossible to hate this guy. He meant to do the right thing. He was trying to follow the rules…and he was still so very handsome. With his hair mussed, his shirt open and his silvery eyes shining a spotlight on her, he appealed to her on so many levels.

Averting her eyes, she scooted around the bed and sat primly on the edge with her knees together. "Go ahead with what you need to say."

"After high school, I enlisted in the navy, mostly because I wanted to take advantage of the benefits, especially the college tuition. My original plan had been to get a football scholarship like my big brother, but I blew out my knee in senior year."

Was that the trauma that scarred him for life? A football injury? She was careful not to sneer. Different things were vitally important to different people. "Losing the scholarship must have been a huge disappointment."

"It wasn't that big a deal. I liked the navy, the idea of serving and giving back to the country that was my home. I had a good life and a happy family. We did okay. In the military, the training taught me a lot about myself."

The more she learned about him, the more she liked the guy. His rejection still stung, but she was already beginning to forgive him. "Where were you stationed?"

"My first tour was on a battleship in the South Pacific, where we were diverted on a mission of humanitarian aid after earthquakes and mudslides on an Indonesian island. The devastation was unbelievable. Houses and buildings were collapsed. The surrounding forest was laid waste. Our mission was search and rescue."

The catch in his voice caught her attention. His usual open expression took on a somber aspect. His eyes darkened as he looked inside himself and remembered what had happened on that island.

She assured him. "You don't have to tell me."

"I want you to know what happened. We were dragging people from wreckage, some dead and some alive. I had gashes on my hand and didn't even feel them." He held up his hand and looked at the faded scars. "We saw a barracks-type building still standing. Somebody told us it was a school. For a minute, we began to hope.

Maybe the kids inside had survived. They might be okay."

She had a bad feeling about his story and didn't really want to hear the ending. But she couldn't stop listening.

He continued, "Inside the schoolhouse, we discovered the dead bodies of fourteen kids, ranging in age from six to twelve. They weren't victims of the quakes. These children had been murdered by a warlord who used the natural disaster to take over this tiny, devastated town. The wounds these innocent kids suffered were horrible, unbelievable. It was sheer evil. Who could do this to children? The inhumanity tore a piece from my soul."

Unable to hold back, she crossed the room to stand beside him. In the past few minutes, the bond between them had been stretched to near breaking but now was strong again. She held his hand in hers and traced the fine outline of his scars. "I'm so sorry."

"Classic war-related PTSD," he said. "My case could go into a textbook."

"Was that the moment you decided to go into law enforcement?"

He nodded. "Following the rules isn't easy, but it's who I am. It's what I do."

She went up on tiptoe to kiss his cheek. "You're a good man, Justin."

Her passion would have to wait, but she had

reason for hope. Whether he wanted it or not, they had a relationship.

"When I came here tonight," he said, "I had something I intended to ask you. This plan might produce evidence that's useful to our investigation. But maybe not."

"I'll do it," she said.

"Not so fast. Facing my own memories gave me a glimpse of what the trauma of your past has done to you. If you're at all uncomfortable with the idea, I'll find another way."

"Ask me, already."

"I don't need your answer tonight. Tell me tomorrow." He paused. "We've arranged a live video feed with Martin Hardy in prison. He's agreed to talk to you."

Seeing Hardy face-to-face after all these years? It would take all her strength and courage to survive. Before she could give Sloan an answer, she heard a hammering at the door to the panic room, and her cell phone rang. An emergency?

When she answered, she heard Franny's panicky voice. "You have to come, Brooke. Right away."

"What's wrong?"

"It's like looking in a mirror. Hurry!"

Franny disconnected the call. Her friend was prone to dramatic outbursts, but this sounded like she had a real cause to be concerned. "Like looking in a mirror? What's that supposed to mean?"

Sloan plugged in the code and opened the door. "Think about it. We might know what she's talking about."

In the hall outside the panic room, Franny stood with her phone in her hand. "Follow me."

They raced up the staircase and into the entryway where two of the three bodyguards had gathered. One of them held up the tablet showing the camera feed for the front yard.

A black-haired woman waved her arms and shouted at the police who were trying to get close enough to subdue her. Brooke could hear her muffled shouts from outside, and she knew what Franny had been talking about. "It's Kiki Galloway."

One of the bodyguards asked, "Should we let the police handle this?"

Though Brooke didn't think Kiki had come here to confess, she might have valuable information. "Open the door and let her in."

"Who is she?" Franny asked.

"Channing's girlfriend."

"No way! Seeing her is like looking in a mirror."

"Not when you get close," Brooke said.

Sloan stepped up beside her. "This might be my fault. When I contacted Kiki's personal trainer, I also discovered that he's her lover."

"Did you tell her?"

"No, but the trainer wasn't real happy about being questioned by the FBI."

Kiki stalked through the door. Her black hair flared around her head. Her mouth twisted in a snarl. "I hope you're happy," she said to Brooke. "He broke up with me."

"Who?" Franny squeaked.

"Peter." Kiki shouted his name. "I never should have cheated on him, especially not with that idiot. He showed up at the house and told me the affair was over. He told me in front of Peter."

It sounded to Brooke that Kiki had gotten what she deserved. "I have one question for you."

"Go to hell."

"Did you have anything to do with Layla's murder?"

"I didn't care about her or you or even this little punk. Franny? Peter loved me. And now he's gone."

"Good for him," Brooke said.

When Kiki lunged at her, Sloan stepped in and grabbed her. With a little help from the bodyguards, he got her wrists fastened behind her back. "You're under arrest, Kiki."

Brooke was almost sad to see her being hauled away by the police. Kiki's personal life was a wreck, but her alibi with her former lover was solid. Her name had to be crossed off the list of viable suspects.

Chapter Eighteen

Another bomb! This time the killer struck closer to home—Brooke's home.

At twenty minutes past four in the morning, Sloan was behind the wheel of his SUV. With the red-and-blue lights in the grille flashing, he broke every speed limit as he raced across town. The message from Keller had come through on his phone ten minutes earlier. An explosive device had detonated in Brooke's attached garage and started a fire. No injuries. The women and the security guards had been taken to FBI headquarters.

"Call Brooke," he ordered his phone.

After five rings, it went to voice mail, and he left a third message for her. "I'm on my way. Call me back."

At the most, it would take ten more minutes to get to headquarters. Not soon enough! He needed to know that she was all right. A fire at her house represented one of the worst things that could happen to Brooke. She loved that place and had carefully arranged every detail, from the triple-pane windows and the marble-topped island in the kitchen to the panic room in the basement. How had her security failed? The house was wired with protective sensors and monitored by cameras. When he first met her at Franny's place, Brooke had mentioned the unexplained honking in her garage. But she'd dealt with the problem, contacting the company that installed her security. Supposedly, they'd checked the system and found no cause for alarm.

Suspicious, he recalled that she'd hired bodyguards from the same company she'd used to install her security system. Had they set the bomb? It was unlikely that the installers and the office people and the bodyguards were all conspiring. A connection to Layla's murder was even more improbable. Sloan clenched his fist on the steering wheel. Why the hell wasn't she calling him back?

Last night in the panic room, he'd been crazy to turn down her sweet, adorable, sexy advances. Sure, the seduction went against his principles. Dedication to his job came first. But she was beautiful, smart and funny. He'd never find another woman who suited him so perfectly. Why had he said no? Clearly, he was an idiot. As soon as this investigation was over, he'd book a penthouse suite in an excellent hotel, fill it with roses and carry her over the threshold. That day couldn't come soon enough.

His phone rang and told him that he had a call from an unknown person. He answered.

A male voice said, "It's me. Don't hang up."

"Who the hell is this?" He swerved around a bread truck on the highway. Two more exits, and he'd be at headquarters.

"Nick Brancusi," the caller said. "I've got something important to tell you."

"Did you hear about the bomb?"

"You bet I did. Sometimes I monitor the police scanner," he said. "And there's already a breaking news segment on the local television stations. There were dozens of trucks and cameramen outside Brooke's house. Most of them were asleep but they were in the right place at the right time to get the story."

Taking pictures of a burning house was an odd idea of being in the right place. "Why did you call me?"

"I've done projects with some of the local film people. You know how it is with us professionals. Anyway, I've been researching experts with fireworks and explosives. It's amazing what these guys can do with timers. I can give you names."

Brancusi was an ass. How could he think that his resources were equivalent to those of the FBI? Though tempted to tell this jerk to bug off, Sloan knew better than to slam the door on anybody offering information. "Text me the names."

"Let's meet. I need a little something from you."

"Kind of busy here." He spun onto the exit ramp at seventy-five miles per hour.

"First, I want to know if the girls are going to Megan's house."

"I don't have that information," Sloan said.

"So you don't think they're headed there. They could be taken to an FBI safe house," Brancusi said with a note of triumph. "Give me an idea where it is."

"Seriously? Do you expect me to give you the address of a safe house?"

"Never hurts to ask. You're on your way to headquarters, right?"

"How do you know?"

"I've been tailing you for the past couple of miles. You're not a great driver."

"I'm hanging up," Sloan said. "Text me the names or not, it's up to you."

Sloan disconnected the call. At headquarters, he used his pass to get past the guardhouse at the entry and access the underground parking, where he pulled into a slot. Brooke still hadn't called him back, and he couldn't help worrying as he ducked into an elevator.

From the glass-walled conference room near SAC Keller's office, he heard several people talking at once. Peeking around the corner, he saw little Emily sitting cross-legged outside the room with a coloring book open on the carpet in front of her. She sighted him, waved, bounced to her feet and charged in his direction. Sloan caught her under the arms, lifted her in the air and whirled in a circle.

After her giggles subsided, Emily stayed in his arms. She rested her head on his shoulder and nuzzled her curly black hair against his chin. "There was a fire," she said, "and firemen."

"Are you okay?"

"I guess so." She frowned. "My mommy is really mad, though. She wants to go home to our house and the agent man says no."

"What do you want, Emily?"

"A Dalmatian puppy with spots."

"Like the dogs that ride on fire trucks," he said.

"Cartoon doggies."

He didn't know much about four-year-olds, but Emily didn't seem to be traumatized by the bomb and the fire. Long-term effects were possible, but this little girl wasn't exhibiting the typical symptoms of fear. It wouldn't hurt to check in with a child psychologist, but Emily seemed like a smart, secure kid.

Still holding her, he walked along the corridor outside the glass room where four women with black hair and blue eyes confronted Keller and two other agents. The three bodyguards from the security firm stood against the far wall. Though Sloan hadn't made a peep, Brooke spun around as though she sensed him. Their gazes linked through the glass, and a quick smile slid across her mouth.

His tension eased. His worries abated. She was okay. He grinned back at Brooke and spoke to the child in his arms. "Should we go in there and straighten those people out?"

"Yes," she said with a huge nod of her head. "They are all talking at one time."

"And that's got to stop."

When he entered the room, Franny approached and wrapped them both in a hug. In contrast to Emily, Franny's insecurities were painfully evident. Her eyes darted, and her hands trembled. When she spoke, her voice was more high-pitched than usual. "I talked to Peter Channing," she said. "I told him I was sorry about his wedding falling apart."

He hadn't erased Channing's name from the list of suspects. In spite of his alibis, he seemed like the most likely person to make the weird phone calls to Franny. "Did you talk about anything else?"

"He told me he didn't call and upset me. Crossed his heart and hoped to die."

"Did you believe him?"

"Maybe." She took Emily from his arms. "I'm going to take this one and find something to eat. Would you like that, Em?"

"Aunt Franny is the best."

Sloan was glad to see one of the agents follow

them, making sure that Franny didn't get lost and start setting off alarms. He edged into a vigorous three-way conversation with Brooke, Megan and SAC Keller. Megan wanted to go home, taking one of the bodyguards with her. Keller pushed for a safe house where he could keep track of all of them. Brooke tried politely to interrupt these two opinionated adversaries but was clearly at the end of her patience.

"Quiet," she said. "Both of you."

"You're not the boss," Megan said. "We're grown-up now."

"I have two reasons why going to your house is a bad idea. Number one should be obvious, but I'll say it anyway. My security is far better than yours, but someone managed to plant a bomb. Your house might also be booby-trapped."

Megan started to speak but closed her mouth.

"Number two," Brooke said in her organized fashion, "we need new bodyguards."

"Why?" Megan demanded.

"Sorry, guys," Brooke said to the three men standing by the wall. "I have no complaints about your work. When the bomb exploded, you acted quickly and efficiently to evacuate all of us. Your driving skills are excellent. And you're friendly, which is a bonus."

"What's the problem?" Megan asked.

"I hired them through the same security firm that set up the system in my house. That system was breached and a bomb planted, which means they must have made a number of errors. We won't know for sure until we have forensic reports from the bomb squad." She asked Keller, "How long will that take?"

"Several hours," he said. "At the moment, all we know is that the device was located in the garage. The room that was most severely damaged by the fire was the office."

Another bomb in an office? Sloan began to see a pattern forming. The bomber seemed to focus more on destroying paperwork than on hurting anyone. He remembered Brooke's quick actions when the bomb exploded in Layla's apartment. Had she done the same this time?

He leaned close to her and quietly said, "Did you manage to save anything?"

"Thumb drives, a laptop and my gun."

She gestured toward a large leather briefcase on the table. Apparently, she needed something more substantial than her fanny pack to carry her Glock. If the gun was in the briefcase, he had to give her credit for bullying her way past security at the FBI headquarters. Brooke was a force to be reckoned with.

She addressed Keller. "As you know, we have experience with staying in safe houses, and I speak for all of us when I say that we'd rather not do that again. We've found the accommodations to be adequate, but a safe house—by its very nature—is restrictive."

"I hate those places," Moira said, speaking up for the first time. "There's no privacy. And I can't come and go when I want."

"It's a terrible environment for my daughter," Megan said. "I want her to be in the safest place possible. But she needs to feel free. A little girl needs—"

"Ladies, please," Keller interrupted. "I appreciate your issues. And Brooke makes some very cogent arguments. Now, I need solutions."

Brooke made eye contact with him. "A hotel."

While the twins enthusiastically confirmed her idea, Sloan held her gaze. In the midst of chaos, they communicated on a secret, sensual level. In his imagination, he was already in that hotel room with Brooke. Her black hair fanned out across a gleaming white pillowcase. She wore nothing but a lacy bra and a smile, and then he'd unfasten the bra.

"It's settled," Keller said. "I can recommend several hotels that we work with, but you'll have to pick up the tab."

"No problem," Megan said. "Brooke will pay up front, and our attorney will reimburse her."

Brooke lowered her gaze and nodded agreement. As they left the conference room, she stopped and stood beside him. It took all his will-power not to gather her into his arms and taste her lips.

"I was worried," he said. "When you listen to your phone messages, you're going to hear me begging—over and over—for you to call."

"You must have been really upset." She stroked his bare arm. "Just a T-shirt? You didn't stop to put on a suit."

On his way out the door of his apartment, he'd grabbed what was handy, which meant jeans and a T-shirt. "I'm glad I remembered to put on any clothes at all."

"I wouldn't mind if you showed up nude, but the guard at the door probably would have stopped you."

"Or not. If I was naked, he'd be able to see that I wasn't carrying a weapon."

She took a step toward the exit. "Here's the deal, Sloan. I want this monster caught and locked up. And I'll do anything to help. Last night, you asked me to make a decision."

He waited for her answer.

"I'll do it," she said. "As soon as you can arrange it, I'll talk to Martin Hardy."

AFTER A SURPRISINGLY relaxing morning at the hotel, Brooke returned to FBI headquarters with Sloan. They were seated side by side in an anonymous beige room with a table. The large screen on the wall in front of them showed the FBI logo with the striped shield, the scales of justice and the banner with three words: fidelity, bravery and integrity. Four technicians were also in the room, and she was aware of at least one camera lens pointed at her.

"Do you like the hotel?" Sloan asked, making an obvious attempt to get her to relax.

"It's not five stars," she replied, "but it's nice, clean and more luxurious than places I usually stay. We have a suite with four separate bedrooms that open into a central space with a table and sitting area."

"Room service?"

"We're taking advantage of all the amenities. We haven't placed an order for oysters and strawberries—not yet, anyway—but we're well fed and everybody gets exactly what they want. It's easier than being at my house, but I miss my kitchen. I can't wait to get back there and put my life back in order."

The images of the fire shown on television had been an appalling vision of leaping flames and gushing black smoke against the thinning darkness of a predawn sky. The fire department had responded quickly, and it looked like the north end of the house had been spared. Her office had been destroyed, and she'd lost many of the projects she'd been working on.

"There's a pool at the hotel," he said. "Did you go for a swim?"

"You don't have to make small talk to comfort me. I had a massage this morning and a manicure. I'm as calm as I'm going to be." Not exactly Zen, but she wasn't hysterical. Facing Martin Hardy was a nightmare that might launch her into a panic attack. "Have you heard anything from the bomb squad investigating the explosion?"

"The device was hidden in the ceiling above the garage, and it could have been placed there at any time. The bomber might have reached the ceiling by standing on the hood of your car."

"That would cause the car alarm to engage and the beeping to start." She should have been more thorough when she checked her car. Her first thought had been a malfunction of the vehicle. She'd called the security service to take a look at the garage, but they hadn't found anything. "What else?"

"The device was triggered by a call from a cell phone."

No help in pinpointing the location of the bomber. "He could have made the call from anywhere."

"Preliminary findings from the investigators indicate that this device and the one in Layla's office were different designs but made by the same individual. They don't know the identity of the technician who created these bombs, but he or she is skilled, professional and probably expensive."

"Peter Channing probably couldn't afford to

hire a bomb maker. I don't know much about Doyle's finances, but he might be secretly rich. Brancusi could afford it."

"He called me this morning," Sloan said. "He said he had leads on bomb makers."

"A guilty admission?"

"Or a stupid one."

One of the technicians took off his earphones and said, "We can start the live feed as soon as you're ready."

Her stomach dropped. She glanced at Sloan and whispered, "Don't leave me."

"I'm right here. Whenever you want to end the session, just say so."

"Ready," she said.

The FBI logo disappeared. The face of Martin Hardy filled the screen. He wore a muddy gray jumpsuit over a white T-shirt. His uniform must have been jumbo, because he'd gained enough weight to be an elephant. He had four chins, all covered with smudgy gray stubble. His close-set eyes squinted at the camera as though he could see her through the lens.

He licked his lips. "Are you there, Brooke? Did you miss me?"

"I am here." She considered each word before she spoke. "No, I most certainly do not miss you."

"You're the most tidy and precise girl in my family. That's what I liked most about you. Tell them to turn on the camera. I want to see you."

She shook her head. "No."

"Please, Brooke."

"If you ask again, the interview is over."

"Fine, we'll do it your way. Now, tell me what you like most about me."

Though it might be smart to flatter him so he'd open up and spill more information, she couldn't force herself to pander to this monster. "Here's what I like most," she said, "the fact that you're in prison and will stay locked up for the rest of your life."

"Don't be so sure, my pretty dolly. There's only a hundred and twenty-eight years left on my sentence."

When he laughed at his sick joke, his entire body jiggled. He'd always been a big man. With the extra poundage, he was mountainous. His beefy hands rested on his belly. She remembered those hands.

Hurtling backward in time, she was a skinny fourteen-year-old girl facing Martin Hardy and making excuses about why she couldn't find his silver money clip. There were plenty of little objects she'd swiped from him, but not the money clip. He didn't believe her. With one casual swipe of his hand, he knocked her across the room. She struggled to get up, but her head was spinning. He kicked her, and she passed out.

Anger mingled with fear as she stared at her tormentor. "You need to answer my questions."

"Ask away," he said.

"You brought other men to the cabin. Tell me their names."

"What for? Are you expanding your Christmas card list?"

"Layla," she said. Speaking her friend's name gave her strength. She needed to make Hardy talk so they could avenge Layla's murder. "She's dead, and one of those men might have killed her."

"Poor Layla. Not as pretty as Sophia, but so loving."

How could he say such a thing? Layla despised him. They all did. Her fists clenched on the table. Every muscle in her body tensed as she fought the terrible heat burning inside her. On the outside, she was sweating. "She might have recognized one of them, and he came after her."

"Not possible," Hardy said. "Layla was always blindfolded, as was Sophia. The men I brought to the cabin were dangerous. That's why I never revealed their identities."

"Why did you bring them?"

"Money, my dear. They paid a nice fee to spend the night with Layla, even more for Sophia, who was also blindfolded. Taking care of our little family was expensive. I needed the dough-re-mi." He leaned toward the camera and raised his forefinger to make a point. "I protected you girls from those men, kept the little ones locked away and made sure Layla and Sophia were masked."

"What about me?"

His mouth stretched, and he bared his teeth in a hideous sneer. "I told you not to look, and I knew you wouldn't. You never broke the rules, Brooke. In many ways, you liked our little family. You would have been happy to stay together forever."

"But I escaped." It had taken her a long time to get up the courage to defy him, but she'd done it. "I helped the others go free."

"Do you regret that decision? Think about it, my dear little lady. Aren't there times when you wished your life was as organized as it was at the cabin? You knew exactly what was expected, and you fulfilled every task."

She'd tried to please him because she was protecting herself and the others. There had been no choice. "I despise you."

"If that's true, why did it take you so long to make your break? You had other opportunities to go. But you stayed."

But she'd finally broken free from his control. Using a kitchen knife, she'd spent weeks and weeks prying apart the chain fastened to her shackle. When she was free, she didn't tell the others. Leaving them behind was the hardest thing she'd ever done, but she couldn't risk having them all caught.

She crawled out through a hole under the linoleum and she ran. With every step, she felt him coming closer. Never in a million years could she re-trace the route of her escape. But she'd made it.

"You liked our life," Hardy said.

"Never."

"Admit it, Brooke, you liked me."

He'd gotten inside her head and twisted her memories to suit his vision of a perfect family of loving girls who looked alike. She'd never wanted that. There were so many ways she defied him. She'd poisoned his food, rubbed garlic on his clothing and stolen little trinkets from him whenever she could.

Rising behind the table, she said, "Go to hell, Martin Hardy."

She'd stolen not only from him but also from the men he brought with him. She'd taken personal items. The memory hit her like a bolt of lightning. This was the first time she'd recalled taking those trinkets that might betray the identities of the men. She hid her treasures in places where no one could find them.

She stalked from the room with her head held high. They needed to go to the cabin. Even now after all these years, the hidden evidence might still be there.

Chapter Nineteen

Sloan wasn't troubled when Brooke insisted on taking her briefcase with her on their drive to Martin Hardy's cabin. She wanted to have her gun, and he understood her need to feel like she could defend herself after her brutal conversation with Hardy. The guy was sheer evil. He'd slithered inside her head and made her feel like she was complicit in her captivity.

Hardy was a manipulator, a psychopath and, most of all, a sadist. He derived pleasure from the misery of those six young women.

On a Sunday afternoon in August, taking a drive into the mountains should have been a pleasure. In a week or so, the aspens would turn gold, and the weather would be crisp and cool, a relief from summer's heat. He drove the SUV on a recommended back route to avoid traffic. The cabin wasn't located in any of the trendy, popular mountain communities. There wasn't easy access to skiing or white-water rafting or craft shops. It was no surprise that after Hardy was arrested and the house abandoned, it hadn't sold. Who'd want to live in a notorious place where women had been held captive?

He glanced over at Brooke, who sat stiffly in the passenger seat and stared through the windshield. Her former attitude of calm was no longer in evidence.

"You did a good job," he said. "When you talked to Hardy, you didn't let him hear fear in your voice."

"I could have done better."

"He's a cruel bastard. None of his inferences that you liked him or were trying to help him are true."

"I know." But he could hear the disappointment in her tone. "On a rational level, I'm aware that there was nothing I could have done differently. I don't blame myself. And yet...there's a niggling doubt in my mind."

"You protected yourself and the others."

"But he picked up on my weakness. There were times when I was cleaning and polishing that I took pleasure in the order I was able to create. Some of my compulsive habits started then."

"Or earlier," he suggested. "When you were in foster care, did you organize your surroundings?"

"Obsessively." She gave a short, humorless laugh. "When life hands you chaos, it feels good to exert some control."

"Franny might not agree with you."

Brooke leaned back in the passenger seat and exhaled a sigh. Mentioning her friend had been just the thing to bring her peace. "If she knew I was coming to this house, she'd throw a tantrum. As far as I know, none of us ever returned. If you weren't driving, I wouldn't know how to find the place."

"Lucky for you, I'm FBI. I know everything."

"What happened to the jeans you were wearing this morning? You're back in your suit."

"Back on the job," he said. "But today, I'm casual. Did you notice? No necktie."

"You're a wild man." This time, her laughter was genuine. "I hope we actually uncover some evidence on this trip. Do you think the idea of an unknown subject is valid?"

"It's a long shot," he admitted. "The subtlety of the murder and the subsequent bombings don't fit the profile of a guy who was so vicious that he scared Hardy. That's the type of man who kills quick and dirty if he feels threatened."

She wondered aloud. "Why would he plant the explosives? Two bombed-out offices make me think that our killer wants to destroy data. Layla might have run across incriminating information of some sort. She was a lawyer."

A thought had been playing in the back of his mind. "So is Tom Lancaster."

Instead of protesting that her attorney was beyond suspicion, she nodded slowly. "I hate to say that I thought about him when we learned that the bomb was planted in my garage. Lancaster recommended the security firm that did the work. He might have had an inside edge, a way he could circumvent the cameras and gain access to the garage."

"It also makes sense that he'd take Layla's body to the mountain hideaway you shared. Lancaster knew the location. I heard him tell you that he'd have the title transferred to your name alone."

"He handles a lot of our affairs," she said. "We've known him for twelve years, and he's gone through a lot with us. Why would he hurt Layla? There's no motive."

"You have a significant amount of money in that joint account of yours." The first time he'd seen the women with Lancaster, they were complaining about how he was stingy with their money. "Your attorney is the one who holds the purse strings."

"We have regularly scheduled audits," she said. "Layla handled all that."

Layla had been shopping for an office, going through the accounts. She might have found something, an anomaly. If Lancaster had been cooking the books, she'd be the first to know. "We'll turn the information over to the FBI forensic accountants. They're good at finding crooks."

"Lancaster isn't an idiot. He'd never do anything so obvious."

"And he doesn't have the skills to be a bomb maker." He remembered the phone call from Brancusi. "Explosives are big drama. Who does that remind you of?"

"Our favorite documentarian. I can easily imagine a scenario where he's setting a dramatic death scene." She frowned. "Too bad his alibi is solid gold."

They rode in silence for a while. Neither of them had mentioned the near seduction in the panic room. There was really nothing to say. Until the investigation was over, she was off-limits.

He kept focus on the case. "Franny mentioned that she talked to Channing on the phone."

"They have a very strange relationship. When they were kids, they played together all the time. A bond was formed. After we escaped, she refused to say his name. On two occasions in the courthouse, we saw him. Franny wept."

"Did he make those phone calls? It seems like something a kid would do."

"Like crank calls," she said. "It fits his personality, but I don't think he's clever enough to maintain the lie. Somebody else could have been framing the twerp."

The final turn on the way to Hardy's house was onto a two-lane graded gravel road that followed the winding path of a small creek. The dwellings were few and far between.

"Do you recognize the area?" he asked.

She shook her head. "I didn't go outside. As far as I was concerned, we could have been on the moon."

She pointed at a rustic cabin with a covered porch. It was a distance off the road, tucked back in the trees. "There. That's Doyle's place. Pull over."

He parked on the shoulder and squinted through the trees. The old man sat on the porch in his wheelchair. As they watched, he laboriously got to his feet and walked to the banister. Not spry and healthy, but Doyle was capable of moving around. "Should he go back onto the suspect list?"

"I just don't know anymore." She exhaled a sigh. "Everybody looks guilty. But nobody could have done it."

About half a mile farther down the road, there was a gravel driveway that led past a clump of boulders. Beyond that was Martin Hardy's two-story house. Signs of deterioration were obvious in the broken windows, the ramshackle porch and the front door hanging open on the hinge, but that wasn't what caught Sloan's attention. Parked in front of the porch was a brown van with a gold stripe.

Brooke opened her briefcase, took out her Glock and shucked off the holster. "I'm not walking in there unarmed."

"I'm going first."

"I'm right behind you," she said. "Don't even think about telling me to stay in the car."

He approached with extreme caution, opening the door to the van and peeking inside before stepping onto the porch. "Nick Brancusi."

Camera in hand, the filmmaker stepped outside. "You've got to go into that house. It's grotesque, dripping with horror. Even without knowing the history, you can feel that something terrible happened here."

"I know," she said. "I lived it."

BROOKE RECOGNIZED BRANCUSI'S flamboyant approach as a documentary maker. He was gathering bits and pieces of setting to beef up his story. No doubt he'd want to follow her through the house, filming every moment, as she searched for the trinkets that might be evidence.

Sloan growled, "What the hell are you doing here?"

"I had a lead, somebody who might have hinted that you were coming here." He lowered the camera and adjusted his fedora. Still in skinny jeans, he wore a brightly colored Hawaiian shirt. "In case you haven't figured it out, I'm good at ferreting out information. In fact, I have something that I'm sure you'll want to know."

"I'm not listening," Sloan said. "You never texted the list of explosive experts."

"And there's a reason for that."

Sloan gestured to the open door. "Why don't you go inside, Brooke? I'll stay out here and keep an eye on Steven Spielberg."

Before entering through the open doorway, she tucked her weapon into the belt of her fanny pack. It was too heavy. She should have brought the holster, but she hadn't. Inside, she noticed the scuffing noise that her sneakers made on the filthy, sticky hardwood floor. Twelve years ago, she'd scrubbed these floors until they gleamed. The walls were marked with graffiti. Upholstery on the furniture was ripped and stained. The house was utterly different, yet she recognized it all.

Memories came at her from all directions. Battered by the past, she wanted to curl up in a ball and hide from the remembered hurt and anger and soul-crushing guilt. Martin Hardy had done terrible things to them, but they'd survived.

I survived.

If the past hadn't killed her by now, she was going to make it. In the disgusting kitchen, she went to the hiding place behind a cabinet where she'd secreted the shiny trinkets she'd stolen from Hardy and the other men. Channing had said that she was like a magpie, and she had to agree. After she took these objects and hid them, she forgot about them, except for the coins. She'd remembered the money and taken it with her when she made her escape.

The trinkets in her hiding place were pathetic: a paper clip, a couple of buttons, a pen and a thumbtack. Not evidence. These things were useless, which she must have realized at the time or she would have come back for them. Another dead end.

From the front porch, she heard Brancusi talking about his proposed documentary on the Hardy Dolls, part two. Instead of facing him, she went through the dining room and past the small bedroom near the kitchen, where she'd slept. The back door—like the front—hung open.

Outside, she gazed into the surrounding hillside with grasses, shrubs and pine trees—a lovely natural setting for Hardy's unnatural acts. A flash of sunlight caught her attention. She saw the barrel of a rifle.

Brooke stumbled backward into the house. Had she really seen a shooter? She drew her Glock and held the weapon in both hands. For years and years, she'd regularly engaged in target practice, but she wasn't a hunter and had never fired upon another human being.

She peeked around the edge of the door. The man with the gun hadn't shifted position or moved. He was bald. Tom Lancaster. All the clues she hadn't wanted to believe made sense. He'd used the security company to plant the bomb in her house. His phone calls to Franny were a way to frame Channing. Lancaster had killed Layla so she wouldn't tell anybody about the money.

When she looked again, Lancaster had moved. Was he coming around to the front? Looking for Sloan? Without thinking of her own safety, she charged through the door and darted up the hill. She raised her gun and fired a single warning shot.

Her motion attracted Lancaster's attention. He stood and turned toward her. She had the drop on him but couldn't bring herself to shoot. Before he raised the rifle, she dodged behind the trunk of a pine tree. Not a very good shield—she ducked behind a boulder. At almost the same time, she fired her weapon.

"How could you do it?" she shouted. "How could you murder Layla?"

"I tried to reason with her." His voice was so familiar, so reasonable. "Put the gun down, Brooke. We'll talk."

"The time for talking is over."

She peered over the top of the boulder. She had a shot, a clear shot. But she couldn't force herself to pull the trigger.

"You can't do it," Lancaster said. "You're a good person, Brooke."

"But I'm not," Sloan growled.

His first shot echoed through the rocks and trees, then came another. As she watched, Lancaster slumped to the ground. Sloan went directly to him, took the rifle and felt for a pulse in his throat.

He waved to her. "Get over here. I need your help."

There was a lot of blood, but Sloan said Lancaster was going to live, and she believed him. She followed his instructions, calling nine-one-one and gathering materials that Sloan used to fashion a makeshift tourniquet.

All the while, Brancusi kept on filming. She told him to stop. This wasn't a movie. Lancaster might die.

The documentarian responded, "I'm in the right place at the right time. Can't stop now."

"Don't give him a hard time," Sloan said. "He has the last, most important piece of evidence."

"That's right," Brancusi said. "I tracked down the explosives expert Lancaster hired to build his bombs. And get this! The guy didn't want to do it, but Lancaster is his lawyer."

They had proof.

Their investigation was over.

She fired a meaningful glance at Sloan. What did this mean for them?

EXACTLY THREE WEEKS LATER, the paperwork on the investigation was filed. Lancaster had survived the shooting. Charged with the murder of Layla, he confessed and was in the process of making a deal with the district attorney. Brooke had been assured that he'd be sentenced to life in prison.

The other women—Franny, Megan and Moira—had returned to their respective homes. As a result of the publicity, Sophia had auditions for several movie and television roles. She was planning a visit to Denver. Most importantly to Brooke, the repairs on her house were underway.

Sloan had made a date for tonight, and she'd bought a sleek, fashionable new dress in her favorite shade of blue. Standing in the front entryway, she watched for him on her newly installed security cameras.

When he arrived, he wasn't driving the SUV. A white limousine pulled into her driveway. Sloan emerged from the back, carrying a dozen roses in each arm. He wore his white navy uniform.

She opened the door, pulled him inside and took the roses into the kitchen. "They're lovely."

"You're lovely," he said.

"Thank you, Justin."

After she put the roses in water, they returned to the front door. He lifted her in his arms and carried her to the limo. This was the start of a beautiful relationship.

* * * * *

Look for more books from USA TODAY
*bestselling author Cassie Miles
later in 2019!*

And don't miss her most recent titles:

**Mountain Blizzard
Frozen Memories
The Girl Who Wouldn't Stay Dead**

Available now from Harlequin Intrigue!

Get 4 FREE REWARDS!

We'll send you 2 FREE Books plus 2 FREE Mystery Gifts.

Harlequin® Romantic Suspense books feature heart-racing sensuality and the promise of a sweeping romance set against the backdrop of suspense.

FREE Value Over **$20**

Get 4 FREE REWARDS!

We'll send you 2 FREE Books plus 2 FREE Mystery Gifts.

Harlequin Presents® books feature a sensational and sophisticated world of international romance where sinfully tempting heroes ignite passion.

FREE Value Over $20

Get 4 FREE REWARDS!

We'll send you 2 FREE Books plus 2 FREE Mystery Gifts.

FREE Value Over $20

Both the **Romance** and **Suspense** collections feature compelling novels written by many of today's best-selling authors.